I0822775

ADALYND
GRAYVES
CURSED
BY
FATE

Copyright © 2024 by Adalynd Grayves

All rights reserved.

No part of this publication may be reproduced, distributed, or transmitted in any form or by any means, including photocopying, recording, or other electronic or mechanical methods, without the prior written permission of the publisher, except as permitted by U.S. copyright law. For permission requests, contact Wanderlust Ink & Tome L.L.C.

The story, all names, characters, and incidents portrayed in this production are fictitious. No identification with actual persons (living or deceased), places, buildings, and products is intended or should be inferred.

Book Cover by Saint Jupiter

Illustrations by Meri Ceban

1st edition 2024

Reader Advisory

Dearest Reader,

I want to thank you for giving this story and me a chance. That you are holding this book in whatever shape or form means the absolute world to me. Cursed by Fate is a story of falling in love with your ultimate soulmate. The one that is your silver heart thread. The other half to your soul—told through the reimagining of Greek Myths. Before you delve further into the book itself... I want to discuss what you may find in the story that could be distressing for some readers. Some of the content includes (but is not limited to):

· Acts of violence.

· Death of family members and a child briefly depicted/mentioned.

· Sexual content of consensual and non-consensual acts(briefly described SA of one main character while under intoxication).

· Disturbing imagery related to death/ loss.

· Darker themes are present in the storyline.

Reader discretion is advised. This book is intended for mature audiences. Please proceed with caution if any of above might be uncomfortable or triggering for you.

With care,
Adalynd

To those who believe in a love that defies all reason and convention.
To those who find their soulmate in the most unexpected time or place.

This one is for you.

The World of Aetheria
North
East
South
West
Isle of Norn
Uppsala
Ribe
Tyr's Bay
Poseidon's Realm
The Aegean Sea
Portal to Tartarus
Island of Kasos
Staraya Ladoga
Colchian Deep
Entrance to the Underworld
Roma
Arcadia
Argos
New Athens
Grecia
Crete
Pompeii
Petra
The Floating Mounts of Olympus
Mikros basin
Vetulonium
Scarab Seas
Corinth
Endessa
Florentia
Draconos Island
Nomads
Nara
Karnak
Dharkermord
Scarab Seas
Nilian Gulf
Aranlenor
Gilgurash's Domain

Entrance to the Underworld

Marcellus's Farm

Arca

New Athens

Clotho's Cabin

The Floating Mounts of Olympus

Corinth

Endessa

Nomads

Seas

Di

I

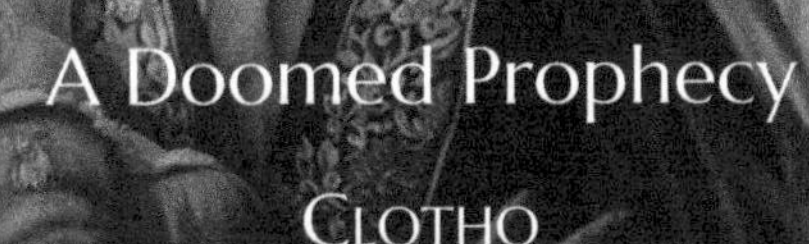

A Doomed Prophecy

Clotho

Torchlight flickers, casting dancing shadows across the cavern walls. My hand touches the rigid edge of chiseled rock. The earth's coolness soaks through my palm, and a slight chill travels up my arm. My footsteps falter as I approach the carved stone throne where the great oracle, Pythia, sits. Her body is twisted from ages of revealing destinies. Silvery lavender hair cascades down the ancient woman's rounded shoulders, past her curved spine, down to her knees.

Milky violet eyes bore into mine with great intensity. Though I am clothed, I feel wholly exposed to the crone before me. I know all too well that she sees past my calm exterior, deep into the crevices of my heart.

Pythia beckons me forward, reaching out with a gnarled finger. "Come forward, Clotho—the

Moirai's time has come," she rasps. "The deeper gods wish to bestow upon you the knowledge of your destiny to come."

Cautiously, I inch nearer, my nerves suddenly alight. Never have I stood before a being so old and steeped in power. The closer I get, the more intense the sensation becomes. Hints of Pythia's beauty and immense power remain even in her aged form. Her silky dress clings to her diaphanous frame. Her clouded eyes become like shimmering mirrors as she passes me a polished seer's orb in her wrinkled hand.

"Gaze into the quartz, child, and see what older Fates have woven for you."

I peer into the translucent sphere, searching the dancing vermillion wisps of smoke, anticipation building as I await the message they hold. The strands twirl together, embracing each other like lovers do, taking my consciousness with them. I watch them getting thicker, wilder, and darker—a vision emerges from exploding charcoal clouds. I'm sitting, a needle in my hands. Weaved threads of reds, purples, greens, and golds lay neatly surrounding me, each solid in color besides the one I am working on. I appear as I do now, but my eyes hold a wisdom, an ache ... I have not witnessed before.

My form shifts, becoming wreathed in shadows. The oracle inhales sharply. "Your destiny is shrouded in darkness, my dear. A thread of your creation will be responsible for a great upheaval in the future—I sense a great upset in the balance. There is chaos, perhaps ruin, and it will be done by your own hands."

I take in her words, but I do not understand them. Disorder and confusion swirl within me as her words taper off. The implications are stark and pierce my mind like thorns on a rose.

"No!" I cry out, the word tears from my throat. "How could I disrupt the weave? I am here to maintain harmony. Please, you must tell me more about this darkness. What else do you see?" Anguish resonates in every syllable I speak. My mind reels, trying to comprehend the vivid yet mystifying vision. Colors are never mixed in any thread.

Questions relentlessly plague me. What was I doing? And *why*? What would drive me to take such aberrant actions? What could cause me to shirk the very oaths I've taken as a Fate?

Pythia shakes her head. "Harmony is not what keeps balance. There is more to it. In time, you will understand. Take heed. Your fascination with humans will be your undoing. Tread carefully, or you'll walk a cursed path. One thread is all it takes. You may face the wrath of the ages over this."

"How could a single thread untangle the great pattern? What wrath?" I ask.

"You'll know what you're doing but will go against your purpose regardless."

I gasp, staring up at Pythia. She must be lying. I know what my role entails. As a Fate, I've made my covenants. She's wrong! I will remain steadfast. We Fates exist to ensure the natural order, not upend it.

Not thinking, I spit out, "You spout lies, horrible untruths! You're a sham!" My head spins as her words penetrate deeper into my thoughts.

She reaches for me and clenches my wrist with surprising strength. "The threads do not lie; neither do I. You saw with your own eyes two different threads combined. Don't deny it. You *will* stray from your purpose and endanger yourself and your wyrd sisters, too."

"More lies! Leave my sisters out of this." Anger roils up in me, only to drain away, replaced by dawning horror as the oracle's words sink in. "But the future remains clouded. How can you know this is the path I will take?"

"Mark my words. Guardian of Fate or not, you will have a choice to make, and I implore you to choose wisely."

I pull, but her hand remains glued to me, rooting me in place. Her voice echoes, threatening to swallow me whole. "The oracle never lies. You jeopardize all destinies and may change the course of the Moirai forever."

I wrench my arm away, my soul shattered. I repeat, "Lies—all lies," over and over. Pythia's gaze locks with mine. There is something unsettling in her eyes—so opaque and solid in form, but I know she is peering further into my soul. I stand defiant to the very end. I am stronger than this, and I won't hear more of it. The orb still rests in my hand. Turning it over, I sneer and drop it to the ground, then turn back the way I came in. At first, I walk, but Pythia's words taunt me in the dark. Now I am running.

The air in the tunnel is thick, threatening to suffocate immortality from me. An eerie presence follows while I continue my sprint to freedom. Tenebrous wraiths claw my sides and tear at the fabric flowing from my waist as I struggle to reach the light at the end of the tunnel. A solid black figure blocks the way in front of me, making it harder to see the path ahead.

What treachery is this? Would Pythia force me to return to her side? I was told before coming here that I could leave this place at any time.

With all my might, I barrel toward the black figure, slamming it down into the soil beneath us and thrusting my way back up as fast as I can manage. I don't look back. I rush into the streaming light at the opening, fleeing the gloom of the cave. Breaking free of its possession of me, I squeal with glee. The sun of Olympus shines down, warming my clammy skin. I stagger forward. My breathing is erratic, but I am released from that horrid Pythia and her wretched dishonesty.

I am determined to keep to my task of weaving and make a promise to stay where I belong, but if I am truly honest with myself ... the oracle's warning ripples through my being. A warning of a time yet to come, a time that will *be* if I don't listen to the lesson presented to me.

I pluck a tiny, bell-like flower white as snow along the pathway. The common folk call it *Woodruff* and say it wards off evil, hexes, and more. May it ward off the pain my supposed future holds and keep me in my place. I've wanted this since I was young. Born Moirai, born to the threads of destiny.

There is nothing I won't do to fulfill my duties. I make another promise to myself then and there: I will no longer allow myself to be entranced by mortals. The mountains are my home, and I need not go anywhere else.

I peek back over my shoulder and see Pythia's bowed form standing at the mouth of the cave, a cane in one hand and the sphere in the other. There is an unspoken exchange of energies as we take our last glances at each other.

I will not speak of what Pythia told me and, by oaths bound long ago, neither will she. I tuck the flower stem behind my ear and straighten my stance before heading back down the mountain.

2

A Prophecy Nearly Forgot

Clotho

The distant past trickled far into the recesses of a nearly forgotten memory. Perched high on the first celestial mountain, I observed the vivid tapestry of Aetheria's human world unfurling below. Mortal lifetimes flashed by in a span of a breath while I remained unchanged. The mountain became a shield for me, a place where I knew safety reigned. But talk of the Moirai circulated among them, anyway. The Fates spun, trimmed, and severed your life thread as they saw fit. If only Fate were as simple as the humans made it out to be....

Still, as centuries wore on, my sisters Lachesis and Atropos grew restless of our sanctuary. Their curious natures could not resist the tantalizing thrill of mingling with mortals. Again and again, they'd beg me to

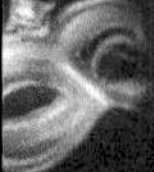

abandon reason, cloak my true visage, and attend the human festivities with them.

I always refused to take part in such fleeting revelry while hiding my face. The words of Pythia rooted deep into my mind, and my distrust for mortal kind grew more each day. So, I hardened my heart, refusing my sisters' pleas. I warned them repeatedly that mingling too often would be our undoing. I had my reasons for declining. They could keep asking, but I would not relent so easily.

Or so I thought....

"Clotho, come. Join us, please! Even Athena is celebrating in New Athens!" Atropos's lip quivers and her eyes twinkle with mischief.

"No, I have threads to spin. Leave me be." I continue spinning indigo threads together while Lachesis's fingers tap the worn table in our hut. She does it to break my concentration. My sisters talk of the traders lined up down the streets with silk rugs, ornate pottery, and yarn they know I'd love. *Don't forget the food you're missing out on*. But we chose a life of simplicity. I have no need for such fancies. No, out in the forests on the floating Mounts of Olympus is where I truly belong. I prefer the quiet rustling of leaves in the trees and the chitter-chatter of the animals to busy, bustling streets.

"Why do you vex me so? There is no purpose in spending time with mortals." I huff when Atropos tries to manipulate me further with her facial expressions.

She clicks her tongue. "If that is how you feel, I am surprised your skin stays unwrinkled. You're such a shriveled up old woman on the inside, Clotho, let go for once! Come on!"

"You are missing out, dear sister." Lachesis's voice tickles the air lightly, her input merely a whisper.

I inhale deeply and hold my breath. These two will be the end of me. We are coming up on turning nine hundred years old, yet they act like silly teenagers. I sigh. I have said no for eight hundred years, and I will *say no* for more. A white flower encased in clear resin sits around my neck. I touch it. *Protected*, I remind myself. But I am unwilling to leave the comfort of our home to test that theory.

My sisters' teasing voices thrum on, needling me like unremitted pests. "You're becoming as shrewd and tightly wound as the old Pythia herself," Lachesis remarks with a smug smile.

I shoot her a pointed glare. Though Pythia and I have forged a friendship over the long years, the comparison irks me. Atropos adds in her agreement, and I feel my annoyance rising. *Ugh, they're trying harder than last time.* My fingers curl around my spindle, grasping it like a lifeline to patience as I direct my attention away from them. I will not give my sisters the satisfaction of an emotional response.

I hear them mutter on about my grand matronly status and roll my eyes.

"You would think she is the eldest of us three." Atropos mumbles.

"And not you, dear sister, if only older Fates saw fit to place her as firstborn." Lachesis winks at her. They are pushing it as far as I'll allow them to take it. A part of me wants to say something, but I stop myself.

I know that mentally I am the crone they often portray me to be, wizened by the ages in mind alone. The blessing and curse of an eternal being. Though they aren't teasing to hurt me, it still stings. *Maybe I have become too rigid? One night won't lead to chaos and ruin … will it?* I shake the tempting thought away. *Humans are not our friends, no matter how alluring their lives may be.* I also can't make peace with the idea that hiding my true form is worth it. I've never worn a disguise like my sisters do.

My sisters plead again. "Please, do this for us." Their voices take on a wheedling tone. My resolve weakens under their unwavering persistence. Maybe I am too tightly wound, like the threads I've spun. *One night won't make a difference.*

Both wait for my final answer, and a sense of anticipation permeates the room as I remain silent. I wait a minute longer, prolonging their torture. After all, they need a little payback for goading me on. I steel myself, my expressionless gaze shifting between them.

"Her answer is always no," Atropos whispers. Lachesis nods in agreement, arms folded against her chest. My face remains an emotionless mask as I draw out the silence swelling between us. Their shoulders slump with defeat. They've given up so quickly this time round. A tiny curl forms on the edge of my lip, but I stop it, keeping my reaction to myself.

They pout with pursed lips and long-drawn-out sighs. I surprise them both when I stand up and slam my spindle on the table. "This thread can wait. Tonight, we dine and drink with the humans. Let's go."

Shock ripples through them both, their eyes widening with surprise, mouths forming perfect o's. Like a cascading waterfall, my sisters' faces pale, their once rosy complexions turning ashen gray. I cannot blame them. Eight hundred and fifty-nine years of *no*.

3

A Night to Remember

Clotho

We debate our guises. Old women, my sisters keep telling me. But I note the celebrations below require masks this time, so I see no purpose in changing our true forms. "No, we go as ourselves and don the masks the humans wear for their festival. No one in this century knows our true faces. We needn't be concerned."

If I am to venture down into the world of mortals, I want to experience everything as I did before I took my oaths.

Lachesis gasps. "Sister, this seems unwise."

"In what way? It's simple. We'll attend their masquerade, blending in with ease, and indulge ourselves for the evening. You get me until sunrise, not a minute longer."

My sisters' violet eyes flicker with fear and doubt. They have gone as old women time and again, not truly partaking to the fullest extent. But I believe either you're all in or you're out. I wait for them to decide.

"Think of the dresses you can wear this time," I point out. "And the masks will hide our faces. We will be fine. I promise. Just keep the masks on."

Atropos nods her head yes, eager to begin our journey, and smiles at Lachesis—her jaw is clenched tight, and she fidgets with the end of her thickly braided hair.

I watch and wait for her final answer, shifting my weight onto the table behind me. "Well?" I ask.

"Such a rare opportunity cannot be missed," Lachesis mutters under her breath.

"Then let's leave at once." I walk to the door, Atropos following close behind. Hesitation holds Lachesis back, her limbs rigid, before she shuffles forward. There seem to be words hanging on the edge of her tongue, but she doesn't speak them out in the open.

Turning back, I give her a reassuring smile. Uncertainty creases her brow, so I pull the door open and stride out, showing her my resolve.

"Come on, Lachesis." Atropos sprints to her side and tugs at her arm. Lachesis keeps her sights on me, her eyes narrowing.

"Better come now before I change my mind." I arch an eyebrow and smirk in her direction.

She edges slowly to the door, Atropos pulling her by the wrist. I don't wait for either of them, heading down the path into Olympus. We will need to travel from there down to the mortals' domain. Down to the city of New Athens.

I thought Lachesis would change her mind, but now we are dressing ourselves in three beautiful gowns, all purchased from a merchant I've monitored for some time. Phoebe—she weaves the best fabric around, and I can't help but keep an eye out for a fellow weaver, especially one who asks for my blessings while they work so hard.

Atropos teases me for watching the human world. "I do it from a safe distance," I remind her. She rolls her eyes before pulling golden gloves over each of her dainty fingers. Her dress is the same color as the gloves, bold and bright—it fits her perfectly and makes her violet eyes pop. Lachesis chooses a dusty lavender gown with silver embroidery. While the choice is subtle, she looks stunning.

The frock chosen for me is not something I have ever considered wearing. It is a gradient of oranges, light at first, fading in darker tones, and it makes my aqua blue eyes stand out. Phoebe and Atropos won't let me leave without it. My mask is a mixture of my eye color and the outfit I wear, with tiny copper filigree. I tie it behind my head to make sure it won't slip off.

My sisters do the same with theirs. I pay Phoebe and tuck a small thread inside the coin purse. I want her to know that Clotho is watching out for her. She's a good sort and never judges appearances. Phoebe treats all that step into her shop as equals. It's why I listen when she calls out to me.

We head into the massive crowds of people wearing their best outfits. Laughter and song fill the air; freshly baked bread and hints of wine trickle into my senses; people sit out at tables laden with cheeses, grapes, and cured meats. More festivalgoers are dancing or playing cards. Fortune tellers sit in their booths with large crystal balls, and street traders hold up fine jewelry and silks.

Everything is so different from the last time I stepped foot here. The world of Aetheria has changed, and I missed most of it. Was I wrong about staying on the floating Mounts all these years? Zeus cares not if we interact with the mortals of this sphere, with limitations on courtship. If we fulfilled our godly duties, then why not? My sisters and I have done so, without error, for nearly a millennium.

Surely, I deserve one night off. It has been centuries since I was near mortals. I am older and wiser. Yet my mind fills with unease.

I brush the feeling off as soon as Atropos takes my hand in hers. She skips to the beat of the music playing, and I can't help but get caught up in the melody too.

We dance, weaving our way deeper into the throng until we reach the city square. Lachesis joins us, our arms interlocked as we prance around. Soon we are whirling along with the increasing rhythm ever so lightly on our feet. Passing revelers applaud our footwork. Flickering lanterns dance with us as a juggler tosses apples to people in the crowds from a large barrel. His hearty warm smile never ceases while his hands twirl the fruit about.

Further into the crowds we go, and we stumble upon fire dancers swirling bright orange flames into intricate glowing flowers. I pause, watching them weave more designs in the air. A flash of red catches my attention and I spot a man in a gold mask. Before I can lock my sights on him, my sisters pull me back into the swaying sea of people surrounding us.

Lachesis breaks away, and I follow her to crowded tables of philosophers. I see her lips widen with a gleeful grin. I lead her forward, leaving her to enjoy her newfound company and return to Atropos, who finds a merchant selling the most intricate of shears. Her eyes light up as her finger glides across jewel-encrusted handles and sharp edges.

"I'll be but a moment." She squeaks.

"Take your time." I tell her before catching a hint of gold and red once more. I spin around to find him, but spot Athena sitting at a table instead. Her face is unmasked for the moment. She is not worried about the humans knowing who she is. I envy her courage. She notices me staring and stands, heading straight to us.

I stop, and she approaches, whispering into my ear, "Clotho? Is that you?" I shake my head, and, despite my height compared to some humans, she hunches down to hug my small frame.

I know not all the gods hide their faces, but my curiosity is piqued, and I ask her. "Do you not worry about these mortals seeing your true form?"

"I do not."

I bite my lip. "I see, and you trust them?"

She smiles warmly. "I don't need to trust them. I need to trust myself."

"Ah." My gaze shifts down, and I find myself fixated on the intricate patterns of the street beneath my feet. Athena is right. *Trust yourself first*. But the ever-lingering words of Pythia creep back in, clouding my mind.

As the music swells up again, my apprehension returns. Athena notices a change in my expression. Her head tilts inquisitively, eyes keenly observing. "Enjoy yourself and let go of your fears. Learn to trust the wisdom I know you to possess."

Athena's eyes linger on me a moment more. With a small smile and flick of her emerald cloak, she turns away and weaves through a small crowd. She reaches the feasting table she was at and plucks up a honeyed bun from a tray, smiling one last time in my direction.

I mull over her words. *Let go of fear*. Fear that has kept me safe from....

A man clad in dark crimson approaches. Loose, thick brown waves spill over his gilded mask. I see the brightest eyes behind it and my breath catches in my throat.

"Would you like to dance? I saw you across the way and immediately knew I had to at least ask you." He offers me his hand, and I take it. As our skin meets, I can't ignore the spark traveling up my arm at his touch. My entire body is aflame as a wave of awareness spreads through me, raising goosebumps in its wake.

When I glance up, I find him gazing at me with an open tenderness that belies his underlying passion. As he pulls me close, our gazes lock. His irises have flecks of contrasting aquamarine brightening to a rich cerulean. They search mine as if seeking permission to drown in the depths of my own eyes, and I want nothing but to do the same.

When I don't pull away, the faintest of smiles tugs at his full lips, sending a flash of heat low in my belly.

"I'd be delighted to dance with you this eve," I reply, my voice a throaty murmur that surprises me. At the sound, his thumb sweeps soothingly across my knuckles, and he inhales sharply through his nose.

As he leads me out into the sea of dancers ebbing and flowing with the tempo of the music, I notice the rigid lines of muscle across his broad back shifting enticingly under his thin tunic. When he turns to face me once more, one side of his mouth ticks up as he pulls me closer to his body. He places his hand low on my back, and I gasp.

The music slows as he guides me into a slow spin, my skirt fluttering around us. I meet his smiling eyes and he asks my name. Stupidly, I begin to offer my real name but stop myself. "Clo—Cloe."

"I am Marcellus. A pleasure to meet and spend the evening with such a fine lady."

"But you can't see all of my face. What if I disappoint?" I tease.

"I doubt you will." He pulls me even closer and breathes against my neck while he leads me deeper into the crowd.

We twist and twirl together effortlessly as the music plays on, matching each other movement for movement. We glide in tandem, losing ourselves to the magic of the drums. Spinning euphoria overtakes my senses as we reach the crescendo, our faces drifting closer. A brush of his lips on mine sends electricity spiraling from my head to my toes.

The world around me constricts to nothing but swirling colors, and the pounding of my chest matches his. With each fluid step, we become more intimate. My fingers interlock around his neck as we twirl. My dress fans out like gossamer wings, while his muscular arms anchor my floating form.

The longer we dance, the more we spiral toward something deeper. His hands cup my face for a second, and his lips crash into mine. He caresses me down my back and gently combs his fingers through my hair. Every point of contact sends molten longing pulsing through my veins, making me crave more of this man I've barely met.

Tremors run through his frame with each grinding roll of his body against mine. Beads of perspiration gather along his hairline as he stifles a moan escaping his parted lips. I can't help but respond in the same way. I'm nearly breathless as he leads me away into an alleyway.

He pulls me into the shadows and spins me around, pulling me deep into his arms. My face rests on his chest. The scent of juniper, bergamot, and frankincense invades my senses. I look up and twirl my finger around a wavy lock resting on his forehead. There is enough light to make out that his mask is removed.

He has a sharp, well-defined jawline and prominent cheekbones, his nose aquiline but balancing to his features. Crow's feet crease the corner of each eye, giving him the perfect masculine appearance, but it's his eyes that draw me in.

His fingers pluck at the ribbons that tie my mask. I gasp.

He speaks to me calmly. "May I see you?" Even in repose, there is a charm to his face, an openness in his expression that puts me at ease.

Everything in me screams to let him remove the mask. *Let this man see you for who you are.* But I waver. If I do this.... He glides a finger across my jawline, traveling down to my chin. I shiver with delight at the softness of his touch. *I can't.*

The fingers of one hand are unlacing the ribbons, and I don't stop him. The other pulls my face closer to his. I feel the fullness of his lips on mine, and the world spins. I tilt my head back to gaze at him. The ribbons are loose. One gentle pull and the mask will fall. I hesitate, instinctively reaching for the mask, but Marcellus stays my hand. My mask sails to the ground, and I am completely exposed to a mortal man. He sees me. My true form. Does he know I am Moirai? I cannot tell. The silence between us expands. No words are spoken.

He holds my face and kisses me again, each embrace deeper and stronger than the last. He moves his hands and wraps his arms around my waist, and a sensation builds within my core as his body presses into mine.

The rigid proof of his attraction presses against my lower abdomen; I am lost in his touch, and I want more.

His lips travel from my mouth and trail down my neck to my chest.

For a second, he pauses and looks at me. "What is this feeling? Cloe, I must know you. Please, where do you live? I will call on you tomorrow and forever."

My heart drops. Love at first sight is not for the Moirai. I cannot give this man hope. "I—I am sorry. I can't."

"Why?" he asks. The sadness on his face wrenches my heart out of my chest. Why do I feel so strongly about a stranger? I can't comprehend the emotions circulating through me right now, and part of it scares me. He reaches out, but I step back.

"My name is not Cloe." I pause. "It is Clotho." I turn away before I face him and wait for his response. His eyes widen, his brows knit. Then melancholy sets in, and his shoulders fall. He inhales a breath, the truth dawning on him.

He understands who and what I am.

But then he perks up and shakes off his previous expression. "I don't care. This feeling. It's not like anything I have felt before. You feel it, too. This is real. I know it." He pulls me back in, and my body quivers in his arms.

I sense his fear of letting me go. I don't want to leave, but I am a Fate. Love is not for me. I spin and weave many love stories, but there is no such thing for someone like me. I keep a hold on him as much as he does me. His mouth meets mine again, and I savor each kiss, each embrace, the feel of his hands caressing my body setting me further ablaze.

Marcellus picks me up, and I straddle him, the gloom of the alleyway hiding us from the crowd. I could give in to the urge telling me to let him have me completely, but I pause. I want more than the physical. I want the meeting of two souls meant to be. But whatever this is ... *it's forbidden.*

The music plays on, and I know there are people still dancing, drinking, and finding love. I never thought I would be one of them.

Marcellus whispers in my ear, "Clotho. One of the Moirai. I find myself falling in love with you tonight." He kisses me softly. "I never want this night to end."

Halting inhalations catch in my throat. An all-consuming flame licks up my spine, melting my every reserve as my body meshes with his, his fingers slipping deep into the folds of my skirt.

As his fingers curl tantalizingly higher, a needful whimper slips unbidden from my lips. "Neither do I."

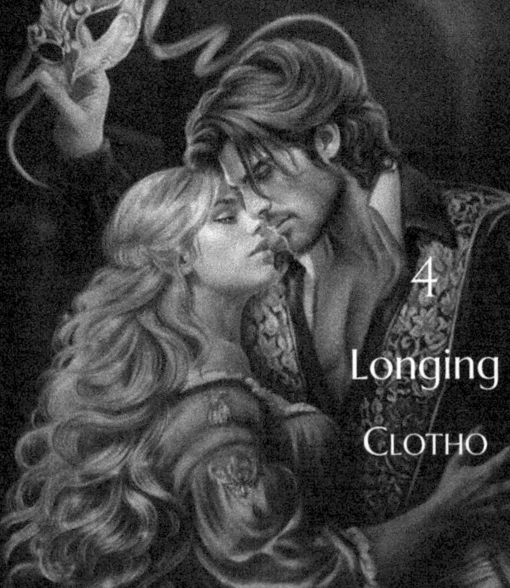

4

Longing

Clotho

The night's memories linger on my senses. I can still feel the softness of his lips, his fingers touching me in places long forgotten. Marcellus's scent is mixed with mine, the sweat from the evening's events now dry on my flesh. I rummage through our apothecary cabinet, searching for bergamot oil, frankincense resin, and juniper to capture a part of his essence. Lachesis narrows in on every move I make, her penetrating gaze causing the hairs on my neck to stand, while Atropos hums a sweet tune, unaware of what's going on.

I sit three bottles on my side table and take a seat. I will have to wait until they are sound asleep to mix them, ensuring they won't interfere with my affairs. If they even suspect what occurred last night, I'll never hear the end of it.

Lachesis's intense eyes fixate on me, their sharpness leaving no room for evasion. "Sister, where were you last night? I lost sight of you after that man in red asked you to dance."

"I continued to dance the night away and enjoy myself. Nothing more. Where were you?" I ask.

Her lips purse as she knows she is pushing me to my limit. I understand my sister wanting to know everything, yet I do not feel inclined to share what happened as I process my emotions. While I trust Lachesis would understand my need, the mere thought of Atropos finding out fills me with dread. I can already foresee her endless pestering. Something I can easily do without.

"I suppose I did the same and had many wonderful conversations with the local philosophers."

"Glad to hear this." I glance up from my work and steady my gaze on hers, resisting the urge to fidget under her scrutiny.

Something flickers in the lavender depths of her irises. Her stare pins me still, my limbs frozen like a deer caught in the open. I inhale and release my breath slowly. All it would take is one second of letting my emotions through and she will catch on to it like a moth to the flame of a candle. I cannot clue her in.

"I see. I remember how much you loved dancing in our youth. I am pleased to hear you had a wonderful night. Will you be tempted to attend more festivities in the future?"

Atropos picks at her fingernails, her attention shifting between us. I can tell she wants to say something, but silence is her way. I take a quick peek at her and set my eyes back on Lachesis.

"No. I've already told you. One night only. And that evening is done."

Lachesis glowers in my direction. I ignore my sister's glare and shift my attention to spinning life's threads. Try as I might, I struggle to bind the threads with my spindle. My mind is elsewhere. I glance up and subtly let my eyes roam about the room.

Lachesis measures threads I've woven in the past, and Atropos is trimming them. I see her out of my peripheral, still oblivious as ever, but Lachesis knows something is different about me. If I knew kissing a mortal man would change me this much, I wouldn't have done it. But I couldn't stop, and I didn't want to. Even now, I long to go back down to New Athens and search for Marcellus.

That idea is far better than the other one scratching at the edges of my thoughts. Every mortal has a life thread, and if I visited my brother Thanatos, I'd easily find Marcellus's. But touching threads already created and cut would mess with destiny. Even though I am a Fate, I am not sure I believe in predestination like some do. The weaving is not as simple as mortals make it out to be. Even the gods are clueless, yet they had a hand in making laws for things they barely understand.

I merely see the life of each human and immortal as I weave. Some would wish for such a gift, but the thing about threads is they are not permanent. They allow choices and change. Each thread woven together is a myriad of choices one person can make. In the end, their paths all vary, and not every life I see in my visions are complete.

Atropos lays fresh cut threads on top of the others in a large basket. Noticing the edges of some bulging out, I get up, take the basket in hand, and head for the door. "I'll take this bunch over to Thanatos right now, before the basket is overflowing."

Lachesis's gaze grows more suspicious, but she doesn't utter a word to me about it. I tell them both I'll be back and pace myself as I walk down the worn dirt path. I take a small peek back to make sure they are not watching me, and then I run the rest of the way.

Thanatos is not present when I arrive. I expected it, so I slip inside unseen. Heart pounding hard in my chest. Though I know it's wrong, I make my way down into the lower basements of his house. I envision Marcellus's face, and a dim, warm light flickers in front of me, then travels down another set of stairs and to the left. I set the basket down on a table where I know my brother can find it. Then I follow the light down into the depths of the Soul Archives.

Shelves upon shelves of tiny wooden boxes greet me. The glow of the orb grows stronger as I approach a dusty shelf with red containers—etched in gold on each top is the magnificent Colchian Dragon, Ares sacred symbol. These are his most beloved mortal warriors. The sphere's light intensifies, steadily getting brighter. It engulfs a box on the top and stays there.

I steady my trembling hand and take the box. Images of Marcellus's life flash before me: A woman gives birth to him in a cave. A large dog and Hecate accompany her, and I sense there is something they are hiding, but what? I cannot tell. Even as I spun his thread, I sensed something I hadn't before, but I would not question Hecate over it as her secrets are her own. And I am not one to mess with an ardent follower of another goddess. The vision blurs and I see him on a battlefield next, then a woman and girl child appear. At first, they are glowing and lively, dancing around a pole as he watches. They are happy, but like glimpses before, they fade out. I see both huddled together in a large bed. Their faces sallow and their bodies thin. Marcellus is bent over them both. His fists bunch up the blankets, and he releases a scream that passes through my entire frame.

I shudder and hold back tears of my own. Sickness ripped his family away too soon. The pains of war still haunt him, and a dark road to death awaits him next. I must keep him from this path. The image of three cloaked figures stabbing repeatedly stains my memory, and the world is bleak without his presence. My breath hitches as I stash the box in my skirts, where I've sewn large pockets. Retracing my steps, I head back up the way I came. After checking the basket one last time, I leave my brother a note.

Before my hand reaches the knob, I witness it turning, and my blood runs cold. *Thanatos is home.*

He steps in and jumps at the sight of me. "Sister! What are you doing here so early?"

"I brought the latest life threads. I left them on your worktable downstairs."

"Ah, that was rather quick! The mortals must be birthing more babies this year," he says.

"They must. I hate to leave in such a hurry, but I need to get back to my work."

He stops me with a gentle grab on my arm. "Clotho, you need to learn to relax. The spinning can wait a minute longer. Can't you stay for a drink with your brother?" he implores.

I sigh. "I've had enough drink to last me a lifetime after last night."

He jolts back. "You went to the masquerade in New Athens?"

"Yes. Eight hundred years of pesky sisters will do that to you."

He chuckles softly. "How was it? Please tell me you enjoyed yourself."

"If you must know, I did. Now, never again. I need to go."

"That's it? No details on what happened? Oh, you were naughty, weren't you?" Thanatos has a stupid grin on his face.

My cheeks flush as I glance away. "No, I danced, ate, and drank like everyone else."

"Oh, sister, many humans did more than that." His smile widens, and part of me wishes I could slap him. He must sense my anxiety on the subject. Every sibling of mine pokes fun at my lack of promiscuity.

His eyebrow ticks up as he waits for my answer. I scoff. "Nothing of the sort happened, and nothing ever will. Plus, you're my brother. That is not something we should discuss."

He rolls his eyes. "Oh, please, we are adults here. We are gods! No topic is off limits. You're a thousand years old and still this prudish? Sister, don't take this the wrong way, but lighten up a little and enjoy the immortality bestowed upon you."

His words sting, but I hold on to my secret as I head out the door. "Well, now I must be going!" I shout as I sprint down the path in between the forest trees. I don't wait for him to catch up to me. I keep running.

The day goes by without a single hitch. It is like the night before never happened. I pat the thin box in my pocket but continue working. Lachesis still seems suspicious but hasn't looked my way for hours. Atropos is silent, focused on chopping up vegetables for the stew pot simmering on the hearth.

Guilt gnaws at me. I feel silly and immature for taking the thread, yet my heart still yearns for the human it belongs to. I feel torn, desire warring with duty. What harm could truly come from one thread? The oracle's warning echoes in my mind, haunting my thoughts. Can I resist the pull of the mortal realm? Or will my fascination upend the balance of this world?

I feel trapped, stifled. I long to follow my heart, consequences be damned—yet if the prophecy rings true, all I hold dear will crumble.

For now, I maintain the facade, hiding my secret rebellion.

5

Summoning Fate

Clotho

Weeks go by, and I still hold on to Marcellus's thread. He still calls out and tells me he knows we will be together, that he will wait until the time is right. My stomach flutters at the thought of a life with him, and I send out a message of warmth and love, so he knows I haven't forgotten him. How could I? Even now, the spark I felt when we touched is still there.

I take Marcellus's box out and remove his thread, holding it in my shaking hand. My memory serves me well; I recall the night I spun it almost forty years ago. Ares was there to mark his box, which doesn't happen often, making it an affair to remember.

Sadness takes hold as I recall the heavy burdens of loss he has carried for years. I am surprised at the happiness and softness that remains in his heart. As though it is a freshly born babe, I handle his red thread with utmost care and let the sounds of the crackling fire bring me to rest.

The embers in the hearth die down to a gentle glow. My sisters are gone for another celebration, but this time it is in Arcadia. *I am alone*. The smell of frankincense, juniper, and bergamot hangs heavy in the air, bringing with it fleeting memories of dancing, laughing, kissing, and more. It helps me with what I have planned next.

As I hold the crimson thread in my hand, I know deep down I am making a mistake, yet I am pulled to act irrationally, all in his name. Marcellus calls to me often. "Clotho, please come to me."

It has been hard not to give into his pleas. There is only so much I can do to hold myself back.

Three days prior, I settled myself outside under my favorite tree. A calm breeze rustled through the leaves; a strange sensation overcame me. Tiny little pricks to my skin radiated all over, and Marcellus's voice flooded every one of my thoughts with his pleas. Even the song of the birds surrounding me became a mere whisper as his words pulled me away from where I sat. Everything around me became fuzzy around the edges. Nothing but tunnel vision. Then a second of darkness. My familiar surroundings shifted, and Marcellus was standing right in front of me. His eyes lit up and joy filled his face as he quickly pulled me into his embrace. His arms encircled me, and I took in his familiar scent while resting my head on his chest. And our lips met. The spark we first ignited blazing stronger than ever. Tingling electricity traveled down my spine and through each limb. I knew we were two halves to a whole. Our very souls connected us beyond the mortal plane.

But our time together was fleeting, and in an instant, I was ripped from his embrace, finding myself once again seated under the tree. Tears stained my face, and I knew then I couldn't live this way. I could not live without him. There is no ignoring this pull. I refuse to endure this separation further. But first I take a single strand from my bound threads, a small gift to keep Marcellus from that dark road and death's grasp, weaving in a silver string to his red.

I am altering his fate, and I know there will be unseen consequences, but the oracle had no answers to what those could be. *I won't let him die*. My brother Thanatos will not reap his soul this evening.

With deft fingers, I ready my needle and weave my thread into his. Ages of combining fibers make the process go by quickly. Silver light sparks throughout, traveling up the fibers, sealing the deal.

A bit of my immortality now lives in Marcellus, and I smile, knowing his life is safe.

After I tuck Marcellus's cord into its box and place it back into a secret cubby in my personal chest, I eat dinner, and grab my hook to crochet a cowl. Winters on the Mounts are frigid and unforgiving, even for Olympians, and I want a head start on new garments. I place another log on the dying fire, igniting its life once more. The crackling flames lick up the wood in a frenzy, warming my face. I sink into the comforts of my rocking chair, fingers nimbly working intricate loops of yarn. Beneath my motions, a deep purple skein glows richly in the firelight.

I allow my mind to wander with the ebb and flow of the hook as it trails whispers of wool in its wake. An hour passes, but I hardly notice, lost in the hypnotic rhythm of the hook's glide and catch. And like that, fatigue sets in. A sliver of my immortal aura is gone, and I can sense the drain it has put on me.

The fire's warmth soothes my skin as I mark off my last stitch. My eyelids grow heavier by the minute, so I set my completed work in my basket and rock in the chair, letting the serenity of the cabin lull me to sleep. A violent jerk suddenly rips me from my seat, and I scream as the flickering embers dance up the chimney. The cottage dissolves, replaced by a shadowy road.

I spin around and see three hooded figures closing in on a frightened woman. *It's Phoebe, the dressmaker*! Her eyes are wide and brimming with tears. *Bandits*. I will not let them hurt her. Instinct kicks in, and I thrust out my hand. Energy flows from my fingertips and slams two of the assailants into the ground. Shouts of surprise pierce the night air.

"Get the thread!" one yells.

I glance at Phoebe, her nimble fingers clutch the strand I gifted her. Relief washes over her face, knowing I am there to help her. No harm will befall my most faithful, not while I have the strength to defend her. I will not let them touch her or take what belongs to her. They have crossed a weaver of fate, and they will not escape unpunished for threatening one under my protection.

I stride on, letting my power radiate out. I face the thief, who remains standing. The other two scramble to join them, but I release a pulse of magic, reacquainting them with the dusty road in an instant. The third draws a crooked blade that glints in the moonlight. They charge forward, and I send out another wave of energy. But they are still rushing me—I see a flash of their cloak fly by, and a fiery pain erupts in my side. The thief wrenches the blade free, and removes their cowl, a cruel grin on her face. I stagger back, clutching the wound. Hot blood spills over my hand before I sink down to my knees.

My vision blurs, and I hear Phoebe cry out. With my last ounce of power, I summon a portal to the Underworld, forcing the thieves through it before it snaps shut. Before I sweep the third in, she utters the words, "Remember this day, the dagger that took a goddess ... *Gods Slayer* is its name."

I waver back and forth, trying to steady myself. Phoebe rushes over, her tears pouring rapidly down her face. She presses her hands desperately to my side, but blood continues to seep between her fingers. What manner of blade has caused me to bleed this much? I slump to the ground, breathing ragged and uneven.

As my life force ebbs, I meet her anguished eyes. I touch her cheek in a final blessing before the still road fades before my gaze and cold shadows rush in to claim me as a mortal.

6

Saving Fate

Marcellus

I trudge along the quiet streets of Roma as they empty from the night's Lupercal celebrations. The city has undergone purification and is now filled with a sense of renewed hope and readiness to embrace the blessings of health and fertility for the coming year. I stare up at the large statue of a she-wolf with two human children suckling her teats. My gaze shifts to the Luperci priests wrapping up their ceremonies. The sight of their wolf masks and fur lined robes adds an air of mystique to the scene. Several of them tidy up the space surrounding the statue, while a group of them urge the remaining crowds to head home before midnight.

I scan the area one more time. Hoping to spot *her*. But there is no sign that Clotho has been here tonight.

One priest dims the lanterns lining the town square. My breath billows out in small clouds before dissipating into the growing shadows. The priest turns and glances in my direction. "The Lupus has drawn to a close friend. Best head home to get your rest so you may greet tomorrow's dawn reborn." I nod and head out. There is not a single nook or crevice left for me to check in the city.

As I pass beneath the stone arch of the northern gate, a chill spring wind cuts through my cloak's thickened weave. I grasp at the edges, pulling the thick material tighter across my chest as the breeze whispers to me. I turn around, hoping for a miracle. *The street is empty.* My shoulders slump, and with aching feet from hours of fruitless searching for Clotho, I finally admit to myself that she isn't here and start the trek home.

The path ahead widens and the coolness of the evening only intensifies in the open space away from the city's walls.

Despite the unusual chill for the season, there is a faint woody scent that lingers in the air. The earth beneath my feet is still damp from the rain earlier. A lone owl hoots in the distance, its night song echoing through the stillness surrounding me. My path takes me across rolling fields dappled with oak and pine. Then the road curves into the woods farther north.

The full moon's soft glow illuminates my way like a lantern hung in the sky. It has been so long since I last ventured down these paths at such a late hour that it feels like I am rediscovering the hidden secrets they hold. As I near a clearing ahead, movement catches my eye on the road.

Peering through the limited light the moon provides, I spot two figures–both women, from the looks of their silhouettes. One of them is lying on the ground. A sense of dread spreads through my body. I pick up my pace, hand resting on my blade in case there are bandits I'm not seeing. As I draw nearer, I recognize Phoebe, my neighbor, down the way. She's kneeling over the other woman, who's lying on her back. Frantic and sobbing, Phoebe meets my eyes and screams, "Help!"

I rush forward and drop to my knees. It takes a moment to process the scene: Phoebe desperately tries to stanch the bleeding, her hands stained with the blood of...

I swallow hard, realizing that Clotho is the one who is wounded. "What happened?" My voice is gruffer than I intend.

Phoebe's voice breaks. I can barely understand her. Something about thieves, a god-killing dagger, and a special thread they were trying to take from her, but she couldn't let them take it.

"I shouldn't have called on her. I asked her to save me." She sobs, pressing down on Clotho's wound. "I can't move her by myself. Please help us."

I remove my cloak and cut long pieces of fabric off. "We must bind her waist and get her back to my place. Go now and bring my wagon. Use the mule—his name is Titus. Hurry."

Phoebe leaves me with Clotho in the moonlit clearing. The sparse trees cast long shadows across her pale form, while the moon's glow highlights the angry gash above her waistline. Blood seeps from it, soaking through her clothing into the ground. I suck in a breath and ready myself to tend to her injury.

I gently lift her torso to wrap the fabric around her. She groans when I do so. I whisper her name close to her ear, and a faint smile crosses her lips, but her eyes never open. I make haste with further wrapping, then apply more pressure with several patches of the fabric beneath my hands.

All I can do is wait for Phoebe to return. I continue to talk to Clotho, begging her to stay conscious. My voice trembles. "Can you hear me? It's Marcellus. I'm here, my love," I murmur close to her ear. She nods weakly, and her arms move, hands searching for the ones I have on the wound. As her finger grazes mine, I silently beg my own gods to save the woman I have fallen in love with.

The creaking of wagon wheels fills my ears. Phoebe is nearby and will soon arrive. I keep myself from jumping up and rushing to get the wagon here faster, knowing that, to save Clotho, I must continue to apply pressure. Blood marks the layers of fabric as it does my quivering hands.

Time slows down as the sound gets louder. I watch the northern road, waiting for them to appear. Seconds seem like hours when I see Titus's frame peek over the hill, followed by Phoebe in the wagon. I yell, "Hurry, get as close as you can to us!" They come to a halt inches away.

"Help me move Clotho." I usher Phoebe over.

"Place your hands like this." I direct her to hold Clotho's upper and lower back like me.

"The goal is to keep her as still as possible." We ease Clotho into the wagon, and I drape my old wool travel blanket over her. Phoebe jumps in and sits next to her and presses her hands on Clotho's waist.

Tears stain her cheeks still. "She's blessed me beyond measure. I had no idea when I called out for her that the thieves would have a weapon meant to wound gods. Please save her," she begs.

"Of course." I steel my lips from telling her anything more. While I am sure Phoebe would keep the secret, I must hide the love I have for this Moira. For both of us. I bid Titus to turn around to go home. I flick the reins and pace just right. Again, time taunts me as I keep steady enough pace to get us there as swiftly as I can without throwing the wagon about.

Clotho moans when we hit a rough patch on the road. "Whoa," I say, and Titus responds, slowing down.

I see the dimly lit lanterns of my house come into view. Almost there. "*Hold on a little longer, love,*" I whisper.

But Phoebe cries out. "Marcellus, the blood is flowing faster than before! What do I do?" Panic laces each syllable of the words she speaks.

I stop the wagon as fast as I can and hop into the back. I take Clotho into my arms and plead, "Clotho, hold on, please. For us, for me."

I waste no time and rush inside. I hope I can mend this stab wound enough to keep her alive. Phoebe comes in after me with a pail of water. She gets it boiling, and we put Clotho on the table. I take my shears and cut her dress up past her waist.

I take clean linens and wash the wound with hot water. I use vinegar next, but I soak the strips of fabric first, then dab. The bleeding stops, but then rages again. I apply pressure to the wound with a thicker cloth beneath my hands. Whatever this blade did, its purpose was to inflict a mortal wound on a god of Olympus.

Clotho stirs, and her eyes flicker open, giving me hope. She reaches out and touches my face with what little strength she has left. "We will save you," I promise, my voice shaken and tense.

Phoebe strokes her face softly and assures her. "We will. I know it."

I am amazed at her loyalty to a lesser goddess, as many favor the twelve. I ask her. "Can you grab my wound kit from the large cabinet behind us?" I use my free hand and point. She opens it up and gasps. "Where did you get this?"

"When I was in the military," I say. "Hand me that powder first. Then the needle and twine. We need to stitch it up after."

Phoebe wastes no time grabbing the small vial of white powder. I pop the lid and sprinkle the contents over Clotho's wound. As the blood stops gushing, I can see the depth of it and shudder. It is a very different thing to be stitching up soldiers versus the woman who holds your heart. I dab the remaining powder away and apply an antiseptic. Phoebe sanitizes the needle and then shows me a silver thread.

"Use this with the thread. She gave it to me. It holds magical properties." She places the tiny silver strand into my hand. I take both strings up and glide them through the eye of the needle. I grimace as I push it into Clotho's flesh. Her back arches sharply as a shuddering cry breaks free from clenched teeth. Her fingers turn white as her nails dig into the table. Every muscle in her body gets tense, and she fights back. Phoebe's hands shoot out and firmly grip Clotho's shoulders, eliciting a guttural moan from her as violent tremors course through her rigid body.

My hands shake as I take in the scene, and without thinking, I kiss her forehead. "It will be all right. I'll make this quick, my love. I promise. You'll get through this. Please, for me?"

I kiss her again and stroke her cheek softly; letting my words and emotions slip right out. I quickly glance up at Phoebe, and her eyes widen with surprise as she locks her stare on me. Yet she doesn't utter a word. She reaches out to my stilled hands and squeezes them. She gives me a comforting smile, silently assuring me that our secret is safe. I get back to work on the wound. Clotho's head tosses and turns with every new stitch I make. When I finish and tie off, her body shakes all over, and she goes limp. I fear the worst but check her heartbeat. The shallow movement of her chest shows me her breathing is steady.

I scoop her up into my arms and carry her to my bedroom, taking great care as I tuck her under the covers.

When I return, Phoebe is cleaning the table, tears running down her cheeks again. I walk over and reassure her. "Clotho will live."

She asks, "Do I need to stay through the night?"

I know she needs to check on her husband and children. "No, you have your family to care for. Return home and rest, then come back when you can. Do you have any dresses that will fit her?"

"I do. I will bring them back tomorrow morning."

"That is great, thank you. What will I owe you?" I ask.

"Nothing." She smiles.

"Surely not, you work hard, as does Alexius. You deserve compensation."

"Clotho is the reason for our success. I need no repayment," she says.

"I understand."

She walks into the bedroom and bends over, touching Clotho's forehead before she faces me. "I'll let you two be alone now. Try to get to some sleep." She bids me farewell heading out the door.

I prop up a chair next to my bed and keep the oil lamp burning. My Molossus Maximus barks and scratches at the door. I go to it and crack it open. He barrels in, nub wagging, then sniffs the air and heads to my bedroom, where he finds Clotho.

He sits solemnly next to her, whines, and licks her hand. "That's her, boy. That's the woman I fell in love with, the one I've been telling you about. You going to help me watch over her?"

He barks low and nudges my arm.

"That's my good boy." I fall back into the chair, and Maximus curls up at the foot of the bed but keeps his sights on both of us.

Exhaustion overcomes me, but I force myself to stay awake. I watch her breathing. The steady up and down of her chest threatens to loll me to sleep. My attempts to shake it off are in vain. The world around me becomes fuzzy and the lamp's glow dies down.

Out of the corner of my eye, a blinding flash of light strikes. I see the outline of a woman near my peripheral. Maximus doesn't bark—instead, I see him let her pet him. The woman comes closer to me, and her voice is soft as she speaks. "You've done well, Marcellus. I will tend to Clotho now. Sleep, and when you wake, she will be right as rain."

"Who are you?" I manage to slip out.

"Iaso."

I smile. "Goddess of healing and remedies."

"Yes," she says as she touches Clotho's forehead before folding the blanket down to her hips.

"How did you know Clotho was injured?" I ask.

"I didn't. It was the love and care you gave her, the plea for her life, that summoned me forth. I also have noted your healing on the battlefront in years past. Sleep, mortal. You've earned it." Iaso turns back to me and places her hand on my shoulder.

Warmth fills me from head to toe. Despite my efforts, I can't fight the urge any longer as my eyelids grow heavier with each passing minute. I hear Iaso talking to Clotho and Maximus before the velvety darkness of beginning dreams wraps around me and welcomes me with open arms.

7
Awake
Clotho

Morning light filters into the room, stirring me from tangled dreams. I open my eyes with a soft groan, my senses returning. Stiffness weighs down my limbs, and a tender throb pulses in my side.

It was as if I were sleeping for an age, trapped in an unfamiliar world where my body floated down a river so pure you could see the opal stones paving the bottom. The persistent ache in my body was the only thing that pulled me back into reality.

I blink, taking in unfamiliar surroundings. Heavy wooden beams slope across the ceiling. I lie nestled in soft, thick blankets, and the scent of dried lavender and rosemary wafts around me. At the foot of the bed lies a large gray hound with a broad skull leading into a blunt muzzle, loose jowls framing his mouth. His fur shines sleek and neat despite his intimidating visage. Around his neck, I spot a wide leather collar and a metal tag that reads *Maximus*.

Though he's dozing, his ears twitch, ever alert to the slightest noise around him. He is a descendant of an ancient breed of war dog from the country of Roma. A Molossus. Even as he rests, he emanates a formidable presence—his half-lidded eyes contain a gentleness about them.

Human snoring draws my attention, and I look to my left. Marcellus sleeps, propped in a chair, his features softened by his dreaming. I stare for a moment, warmth blossoming in my chest. Flashes of the night before stitch together in my mind. The moonlit forest, three thieves, and my dearest Phoebe; blinding pain from a cursed blade piercing my flesh; Marcellus lifting my broken body, calling me back from the precipice of a mortal death.

And Phoebe—loyal, courageous as always—pressing her hands to my wound, willing her goddess to hold on. Together, they saved me. Then Iaso, whispering that my secret is safe with her and to enjoy the love I found. *How did she know?*

As I lay there, I feel only the dimmest echoes of my injury. Mortal and Immortal united in devotion to save me. What they all accomplished is a miracle. I am alive, and the man I love is right next to me.

I try to move on my own, bracing myself against the mattress through gritted teeth as I ease upright, but hot pain radiates up my ribcage as I collapse back into the bed. A yelp escapes my lips as the room spins.

My cries rouse Marcellus. He jolts up and reaches for me. "Easy," he rumbles, his firm hands cupping my shoulders to keep me steady. "You are still healing. Rest. I am here for you."

Frustration wells up within me. I despise feeling this weakness, but the throbbing ache of my injury drains any energy I had left.

"Here, let me help," he murmurs, sliding a steadying arm behind me.

Marcellus lifts me with care, letting me lean on his chest. His earthy scent washes over me as he rests my body on the pillows, his touch so tender for a man so strong. Heat blooms on my cheeks, but I cannot bring myself to pull away. I lift my arms and wrap them around his neck with what little strength I have left, attempting to get closer. His breath warms the side of my face as his lips touch my skin.

He eases his arm out from around me and kisses my forehead. "I will fix us some breakfast. Be right back." He stops a second at the foot of the bed and scratches behind Maximus's ears. "Take care of her, boy." Maximus perks up and licks Marcellus's hand before he leaves the room.

Maximus scoots closer to me, resting his massive head near my side. His steady gaze meets mine, and an invisible tether of understanding passes between us. He senses my divine nature and ducks his head into a bow. I lower mine next, returning the gesture. I am moved by the respect afforded to me by such a noble creature.

I reach out, running my fingers through his coarse fur. Most of him is bristly in texture, but his ears are silken and smooth to the touch. Never have I interacted this closely with a dog. Maximus's tranquil aura puts me at ease. Despite the persistent pain radiating through my side, his nearness imparts a sense of calm that helps me take each breath in stride.

I continue stroking his fur, marveling at the sensations that change me. My pain lessens, and every part of me relaxes. Mortals have it right: to create such kinship with animals is a blessing. Gratitude swells in my chest for this new, steadfast friend.

I am lucky to have Marcellus and Maximus watching over me in the days to come.

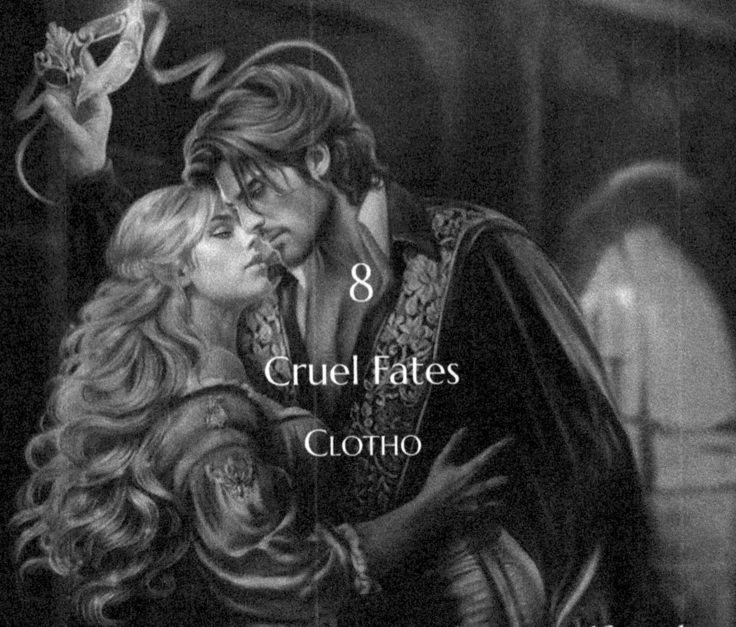

8

Cruel Fates

Clotho

I temper my breathing as I adjust myself on the pillows. Marcellus comes in with a tray of bread, cheese, and dried fruits. He sets it on my lap, and I happily dig in. He chuckles softly. "I bet your body is hungry with all the healing you've done in one night."

I pause with bread in my mouth and shrink down, my face flushing.

"You're stunning," he says as he takes my hand, his rough thumb grazing my knuckles. I love his touch. He has farming hands. He works hard, and it shows.

"Have you eaten?" I ask.

"No, not yet."

"Will you join me then?"

The corners of his mouth turn up, creasing his cheeks and lighting up his eyes. "Of course." He grabs a chunk of soft white cheese, placing it atop a fig, then stuffs it all in his mouth.

I must try his combination, I decide, and take the same to taste it. It is sweet and rich, tantalizing my taste buds with each new bite. "Mmm, this is amazing."

Marcellus looks at me. "I am glad you're enjoying the food. I made the cheese myself, and the figs are from the last fall harvest." He beams at me, proud of the work he's done.

Is this man even real? The old Fates were cruel for putting me in this position. I am plagued with mixed emotions. Do I not deserve love? *True love.* Why does it matter that he's not an Olympian? I don't care if he is mortal. Why is it forbidden anyway? Marcellus's gaze is fixed on me, his eyes filled with unwavering intensity.

"Can you tell me why, when I called for you, you didn't come? And when you did, why was it so abrupt?" he asks, a sadness laced throughout his tone.

"I ... I am sorry. I wanted to ... I wanted to stay but—" I pause. He is patient as I gather my thoughts to answer. "What we have is forbidden. I am Moira. I am not allowed to love for the very reason I am here now."

Marcellus has confusion written all over his face. "What do you mean? I sense there is more you are not telling me."

He is right, and I struggle to answer him. Again, he proves himself—calm in his approach. "Answer when you are ready."

"I changed your future. Last night, Fate had intended for you to encounter the thieves and for you and a woman to die at their hand. I had no idea it was Phoebe. It cloaked her face in the vision. I weaved a thread of mine into yours, sparing your life, and changed the natural order. I've cursed myself and you."

His face darkens, brows pinched. He understands the seriousness of what I did. Before I can speak, he pipes up. "I am ready to face whatever comes next. Now that you're here with me, I won't let you go. *We are in this together*. This is more than desire or want. I know you feel it, too."

He is right. It is like I have met the other missing half of my very soul. My heart swells with the love growing between us. I hear his words of unity, but deep down, I can't help but worry that our time is ticking away faster than I realize. I will cherish—no, I will savor each moment. The inevitable reckoning of my actions grows near, but I won't squander the passion we will experience.

Marcellus studies my face as I do his. I know he is contemplating what I have just told him. It is a lot of information to take in. Anxiety's tendrils curl around my chest as I wait for a response. I understand the burden I have placed on him without his permission first. I hope he understands I chose him.

It could be a thousand years from now and I'd always choose this path. The one where he lives, as soul retrieval from the Underworld would be impossible and I would have to pull him from his heaven there. I feel selfish thinking about it. He knows what awaits him after death. I hope I have not inadvertently hurt him more than his grief has.

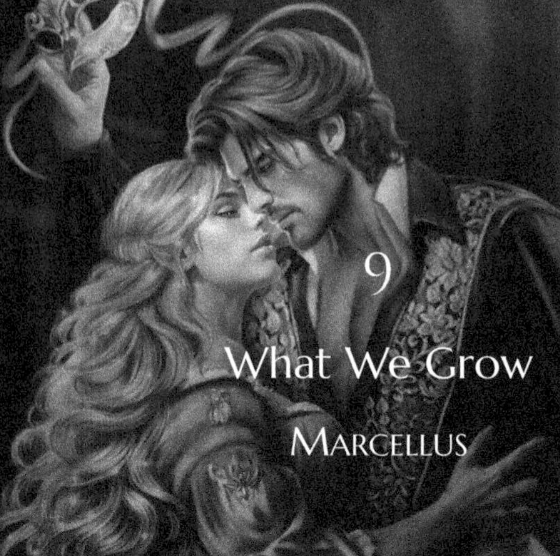

9

What We Grow

Marcellus

The weight of her words sinks in, echoing in my ears as a heavy truth roots my feet to the ground. My heart thuds in my chest as I replay what she's told me in my head. Clotho knew there would be consequences, but she chose love over duty. She chose me. If this doesn't qualify as true love, then what other feelings can compare? The sacrifice she made so that I might live.

I'll go to great lengths to prolong our time together, and I tell her this. "Whatever it takes to be by your side, I will do. Until such a time that the gods force us apart. Even then, I am inclined to fight and stay."

I have a second chance at love and happiness. Why wouldn't I fight for it?

She speaks but hesitates, her eyes reflecting the pain in her heart as she asks, "Are you sure? You could love another besides me, one who would not complicate your life further. Had I not interfered, you would likely be with your family now." The mere thought of me being with someone else stings her soul. It is clear by her tone and expression.

Taking her hands in mine, I choose my words carefully. "No, what I feel for you runs deeper than anything I've known. My dear late wife gave me joyous years, and a beautiful daughter, too. Being that you are the spinner of threads, I know you are aware of my past." I pause, and Clotho nods.

"I am forever grateful for that time in my life. But their loss nearly destroyed me. Then you came, restoring a light and hope I thought I'd never witness again." Warm tears stream down her face; happy tears. I waste no time and wrap my arms around her, holding her close.

I clasp her hands in mine and choose my next words with care, whispering in her ear, "What we have blossomed overnight. It feels predestined, as if we've loved for many lifetimes. Your eyes meet mine with a clarity no one could match. My past was real and cherished yet pales beside this brilliant awakening of my spirit. My family will always hold a sacred place in my heart. It was through them I learned to love from the deepest depths of my soul. Clotho, you are meant for me, and I am meant for you. It is you who calls me home, my missing piece, my destiny."

"And I feel the same, but I know the Olympians will try to break us apart. What then?" Worry weighs heavily in her tone, each syllable emerging tighter and more constricted than the one before.

There is a shadow of dread lurking in her flickering irises too. A gleam of terror takes over and I catch her pupils dilating in alarm. Clotho's gaze shifts off me as she scans the room. I know we are alone, but visceral fear wraps itself around my center. I know the powers of the gods of this sphere, but I have one always on my side, and if I must, I will plead with Ares when the time comes. I also know that sitting with this unease will do us no good. Dwelling on a future that hasn't come is wasteful. We are in the present and I will not squander my time with her.

"Right now, we stay united until they try to rip us apart," I whisper, relishing the sensation of her soft skin against my fingertips.

She covers my hand with hers. Silence passes between us, but unspoken feelings course through the air, and again I am in awe that I get this chance at unexpected love once more. Grief has walked beside me for so long that this gift of joy and love has my chest swelling to near bursting.

When I returned home from the war, the haunting remnants of the battlefield marked my body and soul. I thought life would be harder than before, but I had *hope* and my family waiting for me. Then I found my wife and daughter's lifeless bodies, consumed by a mysterious illness that devastated my world. Death had come mere hours before I arrived and had changed my future forever.

I remember that day so clearly; it was the day I lost all faith. From there, I expected little in the way of happiness. I became content just farming with faithful Maximus by my side, and then I saw Clotho that night, and everything changed.

Her sweet lavender and vanilla scent envelop me as I revel in her presence; a contented sigh escapes me as I experience unadulterated joy for the first time since I returned from war. I press my lips to her forehead. "Again, we face this together. I must tend to the farm but will be back shortly. Rest. Maximus will keep you company."

I head toward the door to the backyard, Maximus close at my heels. I crouch down and scratch his sides, touching his head to mine. "Protect her while I work. Whatever happens, whatever comes ... you must promise me, keep her safe."

Maximus whines, nuzzling his great head into me.

"I know what I ask, but you and I know war. Clotho doesn't. She will need you in the weeks to come."

Maximus stares into my eyes. There is always so much to be said about his keen intellect. A brisk bark of understanding communicates his *yes*. I pat his head before he turns around and heads back to my room.

I step out into the chilly morning air. A new day dawns, and I have more than a goddess at my side. I have true love.

The sun rises further in the sky. I unlatch the door to the chickens. A storm of feathers comes rushing out with chattering clucks. I spread out some feed for them to peck and head to do the rest of my work. Every spare second, I glance back at the house and can see Maximus watching over Clotho vigilantly.

I can see she is sitting up, which bodes well for her next steps in healing. I toss the hay into the horses and mule, and they nicker in response. A few more chores need to be completed before I return to the house.

Titus nips at Cursor. "Silly mule."

I head out to the pasture and take my count of the cattle. The chill in the air lifts as I finish, heading toward home.

Maximus's frantic barks pierce the air. I break into a run, dread pooling in my stomach. Reaching the porch, I find Clotho white-faced and wavering.

I arrive at her side just in time. "I've got you," I say, pulling her into my arms. She clutches at my shirt, her grasp soft and frail. "My sweet lady, what were you thinking, trying to come out here like this?" I ask.

Her voice is meek. “I could see the chair on the porch and thought I could make it to get some fresh air.” Her cheeks are flushed red. “I am not used to feeling this weak. It scares me.”

I brush my lips over hers and lay her in the chair. “The blade’s effect is still in place. Has it done something to your immortality?”

Her eyes flash with fatigue and fear. “I don’t think so … maybe … you stopped the bleeding, and that seems to have been what I needed before Iaso helped. It is probably more my thread I gave to you, but I am unsure what is happening to me.” Worry creases her brow as I take her hands.

“We’ll solve this, I swear,” I tell her.

“Maybe more rest is all I need?” She smiles weakly.

My heart twists. “Let me carry you back inside, then?”

But she is stubborn and refuses with a wavering smile. “No, I’ll sit here a while. The sun will do me some good.”

Kneeling, I brush back her hair. “I’ll sit with you.”

I position myself in the chair beside her, and she promptly turns her head to meet my eyes. “You have my heart," she says. "I love you. I know it seems too soon to say it, but I mean it."

"I know immortality creates a view beyond mortal understanding. But my devotion to you knows no bounds. I love you as the stars love the night. I love you sure as the sun is there, even behind the clouds." I pull her into a deep kiss, relishing her lips touching mine.

We sit, and for once, I enjoy the serenity of the life I live. The animals are taken care of, and the garden is thriving. There is nothing to worry about in these still moments. It has been a long time since I have truly enjoyed the fruits of my labor, and I have the most amazing woman at my side with whom to savor it.

Rekindled joy lifts my spirits once more, stirring a strong hope that, despite what is coming—and it will; I know the gods well, they will try to separate us—but my happiness is not theirs to steal.

10

Time Well Spent

Clotho

Altering threads is forbidden, the punishment should be mine alone, but I know the god-king well. Will I have to fetch the Sickles of Fate while Marcellus faces a test of his own? Maybe I'll be made to watch the man I love die with my hands bound by powerful chains only Hephaestus can create. Or worse... What if my tampering lets loose even older gods? I shake these thoughts off, trying to live in the present.

With each passing day, my strength returns. But healing as a human has been hard work. I have never admired the tenacity of mortals more than I do now. Immortals take the small things for granted. Living as long as I have, I, too, became jaded. This tiny taste of mortality has given me a new breath of life. Some-

times the darkest of circumstances create good. I try to remember this as I ponder what Marcellus and I will soon face because of my actions to save his life. I do not know what tests Zeus will throw our way. I wonder if he will test me further than the mysterious dagger already has.

I am still clueless in that regard. The only thing I can surmise is the blade itself belonged to a fellow immortal and that thief somehow bested a god. I can only hope they've caught wind and deal out punishment to that thug somehow.

I could ask my sisters to dig up information, but I haven't even told them my whereabouts and what has happened so far. I knew I would need to send out a message through the Ether for them or they would come looking. As it stands, they know I am safe and will return home at some point. They did not push me further and for that, I am grateful. Each new day is a test of wills, it seems.

That first week challenged me beyond what I am used to. The simple acts of sitting up in bed, walking to the window or the chair outside were like the treacherous road leading high to the Mounts. Even eating has taken its toll on me. All these tasks are ones I once took for granted. Never again. Small things are everything. The subtle joys make up the richest of tapestries in life, and I won't forget the lessons I have learned here.

Each morning, I rise earlier and more determined than the day before to aid Marcellus however I possibly can, whether it is chopping vegetables or kneading the dough for our daily bread. I have finally managed enough endurance to go outside more. I've lingered in the garden and even brushed the horses.

Marcellus is up early training with a sword. I watch his sculpted muscles with pure grace and every part of me burns with desire to brush my fingers over every inch of his body. A small groan escapes my lips and sends the mule, Titus, trotting off in the opposite direction from the brush I am concealed in. I know it is silly to hide, but I love seeing Marcellus react with his hearty laugh and big smile as he pauses, watching Titus buck around. What a rock he has been during my healing.

I decide to come out of my hiding place. Marcellus has switched to chores. He props up a log on sawbucks and cuts it in half. I stare at him now. Sweat trickles down his brow as he splits the wood next, his face etched with fierce determination. His body moves fluidly with each swing of the axe. Each flex of his bare arms sends my heart racing.

I make my way to feed the chickens and relish the refreshing air entering my lungs. Marcellus eyes me carefully from afar. I squat down to the nest boxes to gather eggs, but my legs tremble some. I refuse to give up, so I push on. He sees me struggling and runs to my side, whisking me up into his arms.

Even though he is sweaty, I relish his closeness and take in his scent. Everything about him is intoxicating, and I love every second. He takes the time to kiss me deeply and carries me to the porch with my legs wrapped around his torso. I could stay in his arms forever.

Gazing up at the clear sky, my arms entwined around his neck, I thank the older Fates for this chance to experience the love we have. Love, I watched happen as threads were spun, but thought wasn't mine to touch. He places me softly in the chair and strokes my cheek before returning to work. That simple touch has me melting into my seat, and a satisfied sigh escapes my lips as I nestle my body into the comforts of the chair.

Phoebe stops by with two new dresses for me to wear. My hand glides over the soft fabric of each. "These are wonderful. Thank you. Whatever shall I do if I return to the Mounts?" I ask, holding the dresses close, thankful for such thoughtful gifts.

"You'll have to come down to New Athens more." Phoebe winks and sits in the chair next to me. "How is your healing? Do I need to grab anything while I am working today?"

She has been so kind and amazing, bringing clothing to fit my size and herbs to assist in my recovery. I can't think of anything and let her know. "Not this time. You have me set up for several weeks. Thank you again, dearest friend."

A look of astonishment and joy crosses Phoebe's face, her eyes widen, and her cheeks turn a rosy shade of pink. "D–Dearest friend? Me? I—" She stammers, pressing a hand to her chest.

"Yes, I may be a goddess, but this doesn't mean we aren't equals. Remember how worthy and wonderful you are," I say.

"Knowing that I have earned such friendship from you is a privilege beyond spoken words! Your divine blessings have graced my life tenfold." She beams.

I give her hand a gentle squeeze. Very few have touched my heart during my life as an immortal. This kindhearted woman's selfless nature and gracious wisdom never cease to inspire me. "I only helped amplify what was already there." I smile, and she radiates pure joy before bidding me farewell. A wide smile and warmth I've never felt before sits with me while I watch her fade off in the distance.

Besides my sisters and brother, I have few friendships, since not all immortals are trustworthy. Mortals are different. Maybe it is the inevitability of death that changes how they make friends? Either way, I am glad that I have had the chance.

I reflect on my time sequestered away on the Mounts, afraid of a prophecy that was vague to begin with. If there is anything I regret, it is not forging more friendships with the humans on Aetheria.

I take the dresses into the house and lay them neatly on the chest in front of the bed before heading into the kitchen. There, I grab some meat, cheese, and bread, wrapping it up before going back out. Marcellus will appreciate the tiny meal I prepped. I sit back down, giving my body ample time to recoup before I head back out to help him.

Marcellus's hands are holding my waist while I reach for apples from his favorite tree. I place each ripened fruit in the basket, filling it to the brim. He helps me down and offers me some fresh berries; I readily accept, and he plops one gently in my mouth. I have no idea why the fruit here tastes better than on the Mounts, but it does. He hands me a deep red apple, and I sink my teeth into its sweetness.

Maybe it's the care that he puts into each plant and animal under his watch? Either way, I enjoy the food down here more than I do at home. But home is feeling less like *home*. Longing seeps deep into my marrow as I wish I could stay here forever. I know my sworn oaths, my duties, but I never want to return. I am content to live here as he does. But the possibility of living my life out with Marcellus is nothing but a dream I cling to.

Pythia's face fills my vision, and I nearly choke on the bite of apple I take. It is a warning of chaos that is yet to come. This peace cannot last forever. I cough violently, trying to dislodge the offending morsel. Gagging, I lurch forward, struggling to get the piece out. I finally feel the chunk shift with one last powerful hack before it shoots out and I can breathe in the sweet air without obstruction.

The message tries to taunt me further, but I ignore it as Marcellus fusses over me. Even Maximus is at my side. A gruff, low woof reverberates from his muzzle while he stands erect.

I stroke the top of his head. "I'm okay, boy." He grunts in response and sits back down.

Marcellus hands me his waterskin. "Here, drink," he says, and I gulp down the liquid with zeal. It soothes the scratch in my throat, and I let out a sigh of relief.

"Will you be all right?" he asks.

"I am fine. Promise," I reassure him. But the crease deepens in his brow, and his gaze is unwavering. I tilt my chin downward in silent affirmation.

Marcellus accepts my gesture and gently glides the tips of his warm fingers across my skin, tracing delicate patterns up and down my arm as I meet his worried gaze. His look ignites a spark low in my belly, despite my rattled nerves. With every touch, a delightful shiver runs down my spine. As his fingertips brush my wrist in rhythmic strokes, my heart races, and the same warmth I felt the first night we met builds up deep from my center and courses through my entire body.

I lean into his caress and let my forehead rest against his chest. He pulls me closer. His continued touch soothes me further and melts the tension from my aching muscles. Safe and calmed in his embrace, I allow myself to truly feel the fondness that grows between us.

The rest of the day goes without a hitch. No more visions, no more incidents. I glance over at Marcellus, who is forking hay out to his cattle. Tall, lean muscles glisten in the afternoon light. His chestnut tresses are parted in the middle, curving down in layers near the top of his cheeks. The style suits him. He pulls his hand through his hair, combing it back out of his face. This mundane movement captivates my gaze with mingled awe and yearning.

He senses my intense stare lingering in his direction, and his lip curves up in a wry smile. I clear my throat, digging my hand into the bucket of scratch grains for the chickens. They cluck near my feet and eagerly peck at the earth when I spread it across the ground in front of me.

He's tracking my every movement now. So many unsaid feelings expressed with a simple look or touch. How much longer will we play this teasing game? I am ready to explode. It is the knowledge of the forbidden nature of our love that prevents me from acting on my emotions. Is he doing the same? If we go further, will it bring about the collapse of everything I hold dear?

The last thousand years replay in my mind. Not all my time was spent as a Fate. My sisters and I ate, drank, and bathed like mortals do. I enjoyed a good life, traveling the floating Mounts and visiting the marveling depths of the Underworld. I let myself love before and had told myself never again. The humans would consider me lucky, but the task of weaving has become a heavy burden to bear, and the gods are a tricky bunch.

The way gods choose to live has tainted and soured my experiences. Except now, whatever this is with this mortal man is so much more than what the Mounts offer. I know my emotions are irrational, but fate and destiny are strange things. Much like Pythia said before: it is not as simple as we make it out to be. There is more nuance. I know this from working the threads.

Destiny is what we make of it. So why must I, a deity in my own right, obey without question the decrees of Zeus, who rules from his throne with one hand yet clutches his lightning in the other to bend rules as it suits his fleeting desires?

As Fate incarnate, I shape the lives of gods and men, yet defer to one whose oaths last only until the next mortal catches his roving eye? Zeus demands abstinence from attachments between mortal and immortal, yet in the same breath indulges carnal whims.

He also cares not if other deities bed mortals, but that is far as we should go. Falling in love with them is not allowed. I've wondered: who thinks about the broken hearts left behind by thoughtless flings? Sex is not without consequence. The many demigods are proof of that. And many mortals and immortals are wounded or punished for overstepping the bounds.

I will face his wrath for what I have done and will do, but I care not what happens to me as long as Marcellus remains unscathed. And maybe this is the reason Pythia warned me of the darkness that cloaked me in her vision. Because love cannot be bound by the rules of a hypocritical play-king.

Marcellus pulls me from my thoughts, and I realize my focus is on the wrong things. I know what the future holds. I need to live in the now, with him, in these stolen moments that are precious to me. A thousand years lived to know what true love is in the end. A bittersweet experience.

11

Visitor

Clotho

The blazing orange sun sinks low on the horizon, casting a warm glow over the edges of the sprawling farm. The light reaches the perimeter of where the nearby forest begins and disappears in the shadow of the trees. Marcellus and I are still outside from the day's workload, and I feel stronger than before. By this time, I am often in the house resting, but I have worked alongside Marcellus for hours without tiring today. The very thought brings with it a sense of accomplishment and pure joy.

Another week has gone by, and I wish to stay here forever—to bask in the peaceful countryside, where time seems irrelevant as we revel in the beauty of cultivating a farm that works with nature and provides such bountiful gifts. I know it won't always be like this, so I choose to lose myself in doing. I choose to soak in every second with Marcellus and the creatures I've come to know and love, too.

Marcellus hauls dead branches into a neat pile for our bonfire. We will celebrate the start of spring together. Clutching a bundle of kindling, I eagerly await my turn to contribute to the intricately built pyre of timber. The sweet scent of cut wood fills my nostrils, adding to nature's symphony around us. Even though spring's early chill has fled, the night still carries a nip in the air, and the fire's embrace will be comforting.

My next task is inside. I step over the threshold, and a cozy warmth greets me with open arms. I get ready to work my magic with kitchen tools in my grasp, my hands moving instinctively, mimicking rhythms established in kitchens past. I quarter up scarlet tomatoes and pour rich wine in next. It meets sizzling beef and softened pearl onions within a broad pot. I sprinkle cinnamon, clove, and allspice to the mixture, too, transforming it into a mouth-watering stew. The savory aroma rises from the bubbling pot, and I can almost taste the flavors on my tongue.

Beside me is Maximus, standing guard while I cook. I gather some leftover cuts of meat and mix in an egg, vegetables, and some blueberries. I lay a large bowl at his feet and watch him dig in enthusiastically. With my hand, I lovingly touch the top of his head, running my fingers through his fur, and bask in the soothing sound of his contentment.

Even with the food in his bowl, he is ever watchful of me since my first night here. He glances up at me while I stir the pot some more and add bay leaves. My stomach grumbles with hunger, but the stew needs a few more minutes to cook. A wash basin filled with hot, soapy water awaits me, so I clean up the mess I have left and grab a large tray, tucking two small, round loaves of bread at the corners.

With a large wooden spoon, I scoop out hearty portions of stew, filling two stone bowls to the brim before placing them on a tray with a small bowl of steamed spinach. I can't wait to dig in. Placing the bowls on the tray, I set them down and carefully tuck some morsels of cheese next to them. I dust my hands on the apron I'm wearing, stand by to check out my handiwork, and add a sprig of rosemary to the top of each bowl.

Just as I reach for the tray, Marcellus slides between the table and me with fluid grace. The heat of his muscled frame against me sends my knees trembling. The rise and fall of his chest engulfs my vision before I gaze up at him. “Let me take that, my lady.” He winks, and with the same swiftness as before, the tray is in his hands and he’s already heading out the door. I am left standing in awe at the response my body gives with the slightest touch. It leaves me breathless and wanting more—no, all of him—against me, to merge body and soul.

With a basket of other goodies, I quickly make haste and rush out to catch up to him. I step out into the cool night, following the glow of the bonfire. Marcellus has laid out a blanket with large cushions and a short table close enough to the flames for warmth, setting our meal upon it with care.

He glances up at my approach, eyes gleaming with joy in the firelight. “The stew smells amazing. Your talents in the kitchen never cease to amaze me. I can’t wait to taste a bit of heaven,” he says, his gaze drifting down my frame as he helps me to my seat. His hand grazes my side to my thigh before he withdraws his touch, leaving an inferno in its wake.

I settle onto the plush cushions, my skin blazing from his lingering caress. He's quite the tease. I have no idea how much more of this back and forth I can take.

Marcellus's eyes rake over me again as the rich scent of wine reaches my nostrils. He pours some into two clay cups. "Try this."

He passes mine to me, and the rich aroma tempts my senses before I even have a taste. As I take a sip, a burst of flavor greets me: tangy berries and warm spices tantalize my tongue. Next, he hands me a bowl, and we dine in silence, admiring the emerging stars in the sky above.

Marcellus finishes first, reclining on one elbow. His lean, muscular frame outlined in the dim light teases my senses further. His gaze is fixated on me with a tenderness that makes my heart flutter in my chest. I meet the intensity of his stare and feel myself falling into the depths of his eyes.

He reaches over and brushes a lock of hair from my cheek. The touch is electric, sending a shiver down my spine as his fingers linger, tracing the outline of my jaw. I lean into his warm palm with a sigh. He smiles wickedly at me, his expression playful and seductive.

Lowering his head until our breath intermingles, he breathes, "I never want our nights like this to end. I wish for them to last forever," his mouth hovering a hair's breadth from mine. The heat of his words washes over me, and a deep need rises within.

"As do I," I whisper against his mouth, craving nothing but his fiery embrace. His lips graze mine with an almost imperceptible touch that still ignites every nerve ending in my body.

"I want to keep you here beside me, and give you joy in every way. I want to become one over and over until dawn comes." A low groan rumbles from his chest as his tongue slowly traces my bottom lip.

My mouth opens under his with a soft gasp. "Show me," I moan, urging him to continue.

He whisks me into his lap and pulls me closer. My hands slide into his dark hair, holding him near as my body trembles from his actions. Marcellus pulls back just enough to meet my hazy gaze, passion and promise blazing in his eyes. "As my lady commands," he thrums, desire thickening his voice before he claims my lips in a hungry, endless kiss.

He pours all his longing into the intimate caress of our locked lips. I cling to him, returning every action with equal fervor, losing myself in the exquisite sensations he draws from my body.

His hands roam to my sides before he takes hold of my hips, pressing me fully against his body. Through the thin barrier of our clothing, I feel his hardness, which sends fresh flames licking through my veins.

I rock my bottom half back and forth, seeking more friction to ease the ache building in me. Marcellus moans at my shameless motions, his own hips surging to meet mine. "You undo me, my beloved," he rasps, tearing his mouth from mine to trail open-mouthed kisses along my throat.

My head falls back as he sucks the delicate skin above my breasts. "I am yours to have. Take me," I plead, uncaring of anything other than completion in his arms.

Before he can reply, a burst of light explodes near the fire, parting our heated embrace. Shaken, I scramble to my feet, Marcellus close behind me. A gleaming goddess steps forward with a grave expression on her face. "I'm sorry for the interruption, but I had to warn both of you. Danger comes soon, and you need to leave this place."

"Iaso, is that you? What's going on?" I ask.

"Zeus is aware of what you've done. A shift in the world has been felt, and he knows you tampered with the threads. I am not sure what disaster this spells for you, dear friend, but you need to protect yourselves, and quick." She pats my arm.

"Iv... I am sorry," is all I can say.

"Clotho, the love you have with this man, it is true. Fight Zeus. I know you can win. Whatever he makes you do, remember that ... please know there are gods and goddesses on your side. But I would hide Marcellus before Zeus digs his claws into him."

"Where do I go? Where do I take him?"

"Go to Hades. He's not a hypocrite and will keep his word," Iaso reassures me, but I am shaking. Pythia was right, and I am the fool. But I still don't know what has happened.

"Can you tell me more about the shift? What is happening?" I ask.

"Rumors are one Titan escaped from the prison Tartarus. Whatever you did stirred up the Ether's energies enough to allow the release. Whispers have spread that it is Cronos," she says.

I freeze and shudder at her words. "This is not good. How could this be? Truly?"

"This is what I have heard. I am not sure, my dear, you're the expert on destinies and threads and how they interact with our worlds, but also Cronos is old and knows how to manipulate the very fibers of our universe. He must have sensed the opportunity. Leave tonight or tomorrow morning. Please, my friend."

"But I cannot ask Marcellus to flee his home. Surely, there is another way?"

"You must leave. They will track your godsaura. I must go now, before they sense I have left the Mounts. I wish you both the best. It was lovely to see you again, Marcellus." She nods slightly in his direction and smiles. He returns the gesture. Before I can ask how they know each other, she fades into the dark fringes outside the boundary of the bonfire.

"Iaso spoke with you so familiarly. Is she a matron goddess of yours?" I ask as soon as I turn around, facing Marcellus.

His gaze drifts off toward the fire as he speaks, "When I was tending your wound that night you were stabbed, I was desperate for help, and she appeared in a flash of light and told me she would take care of the rest. She said she saw me healing soldiers and noted my skills and compassion. She stayed to ensure you recovered."

I thought she came to me of her own volition and never felt the need to ask Marcellus about it. This man never ceases to amaze me with his gifts. For Iaso to come to any mortal is hard won, not a task done carelessly. No, she was already aware of the lengths he'd go to help and heal.

"Anything else you want to know about that night?" he asks.

"No, I am grateful for you both. Iaso is a dear friend. I am in awe of her ability to keep my secrets. Not even my sisters know exactly where I am. I asked them to stay away because I didn't want their involvement to cause issues later, but soon they will come looking for me, and I must answer for what I have done."

"The mixing of our threads?"

I nod, dread pooling in my stomach. "Yes—oh, what have I done? I'm so sorry I've doomed us both to a Fate worse than death. Zeus will show no mercy if he discovers who you are." I sink into his embrace, tears spilling as he holds me firm in his arms.

I let myself feel everything for once as the tears continue. I knew this was coming, but I wished it had been much later. All I want is more time with Marcellus before we face the biggest test of our lives together.

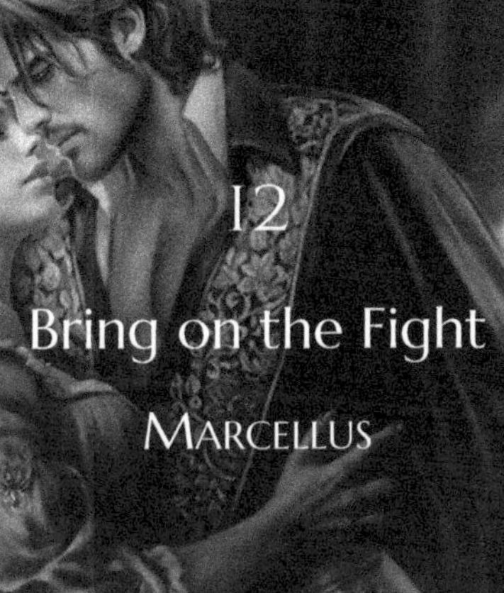

12

Bring on the Fight

Marcellus

Clotho trembles against my chest as her sobs reverberate through me. My throat tightens, and a fierce want to take away her pain overcomes me. She speaks of leaving, and dread like no other grips my heart. "If you depart alone, will I see you again? I refuse to lose you a second time. I can't." The thought has my heart constricting with dread. She's the one thing I can't bear to lose, especially after everything else I've lost.

"I do not know, but your safety is all that matters, you and Maximus." Her words are weak as more tears spill down her cheeks.

"No, I don't like this idea. There's another way, I'm sure."

The moment Clotho revealed who she was, I knew what I signed up for. Even after calling out for her after that night and the days that followed, there was a part of me that thought I'd never see her again—yet somewhere deep down, a knowing grew, and I waited. Patience was my friend until that fateful night when a thug tried to rip her immortality away. I tug her closer against me. She shakes in silence, and my emotions threaten to overwhelm me. Separation weighs heavily on my mind now.

My emotions churn inside like a raging sea of waves crashing over me, threatening to consume me whole. Memories of war and family loss still haunt my mind, but they do not compare to the longest night of my life, seeing her lying there, her soul draining away. My racing thoughts of *not again, don't let it end this way*. The helplessness that swallowed me whole before Iaso arrived.

I fear I will not survive a second blow to my heart. I'd become an empty shell. Devoid of all feeling and purpose.

I am merely a mortal man. We both know this. No matter how much I may try, I cannot defeat Zeus alone. Still, I have favor with other gods, and things owed to me. I'd fight a thousand battles and lose if it meant I could be with her forever.

"I am ready to do whatever it takes to stay together." I tell her, but I can see she is afraid.

"You do not know them like I do," she says.

"Help me understand, then."

"Iaso is right. Hades is our only chance, but if we go together and Zeus catches us first..." She pauses. "I fear what he will do to you. He'd gladly rip you from my arms."

I cup her cheek and tilt her chin so her tear-filled eyes meet mine. "Do not fear for me, my love. While I am mortal, I will fight and best death to return to your side. No god's wrath can destroy the bond we share. I love you, Clotho of the Moirai. I love you now and always."

Her tears still stream freely down her face. "And I love you. Your safety is my only concern. I feel the shadows pressing in on us. I can't bear the thought of losing you."

I glide my finger along her jaw, memorizing every contour as if it is the last time I'll caress her soft skin.

"No force in this realm or the next can break what we have. I am ready to fight for our love."

"Then we need to stagger the times we leave. I can head out first. You can follow an hour after. It should give us some advantage over those who interfere. Stop for no one. I will direct you to the Underworld. Once there, head straight to the Ferryman Kharon. Shake his hand so he can sense that I have sent you. Give me your hand." She takes my hand in hers. I stare down, puzzled at what she is doing. Little fiery sparks trickle across my skin; a design of gold etches in and disappears as quickly as it popped up.

Then she touches her index finger to my forehead. A vision disables my ability to see what's around me. The path to the Underworld lies ahead, a winding path through trees in the woods west of here. The air is thick, filled with an otherworldly energy that leaves my skin tingling. More details are shown to me. I commit them to memory. I know where I must go. My sight returns, and she is standing there, patience in her eyes, waiting for me to respond.

I hastily pull her close and kiss her again. Even though there is still plenty of time until morning, I know it is better for us to sleep. “How I want to have all of you this eve, but I fear we need our sleep. You, most of all, need the rest before this journey.”

She tugs gently at my bottom lip with her teeth. “I am healed, my love. I’d rather stay awake and savor the last few hours we have alone.”

“Are you sure?” I ask.

“Yes,” she says, but I am not convinced. We still know nothing about the blade that wounded her. Goddess or not. Even now, I can see the war inside her eyes. She is questioning how to proceed like me.

The night’s energy shifts around us, and I take her up into my arms. She wraps her legs around me. I want nothing more but to lay her down and make love to her. Maximus’s hair bristles up and a low growl deep from his chest rolls out. I sense we are not alone and whisk them both inside. “Hurry back to the house.” I do not know what my faithful hound senses, but the hairs on my neck are erect and Clotho grows eerily quiet. It is like there are a hundred eyes peering at us from the depths of the dark.

“What is this that fills me with dread?” I ask.

"I–I am unsure." Clotho's voice shakes. "But we need to leave as soon as light touches the night sky."

"Then we must choose rest."

I guide her to the bed and settle her in, joining her side, tucking my arm behind her. I tell myself I have time yet, that we will solidify our bond once we are safe in the Underworld and not in the hands of those who would side with Zeus so easily.

I am not foolish. I know the many fathered demi-gods that are Zeus's sons and daughters. Even some beasts on Aetheria readily answer his call.

Ares, please don't fail me. I plead. Please grant us safe passage.

Cloth sighs softly as she settles against me, her body relaxing into mine. A small smile crosses my mouth and I brush my lips across her cheek. She snuggles deeper into my chest, her eyes closing. I knew she was tired from the day's events. I drift in and out of consciousness, yet the warmth of her body against mine lolls me into a lucid slumber.

Early morning light peeks in through the window. Maximus nudges my hand and I get up, dreading what I must do next. I remind myself this is not a permanent separation. I grasp Clotho's hand in mine and whisper. "The light has come. We must get ready to leave, my love."

Her eyelids stir, and she groans, grabbing the covers and pulling them up to her chin. I don't blame her. While we both slept, I cannot say it was a restful sleep that rejuvenates. No, it was plagued with nightmares and more. The only good thing was having Clotho next to me.

She tugs at my wrist and pulls me close to her face next. "I wish we didn't have to do this," she says.

"I know."

She warily gets out of bed and heads to the washroom for fresh clothes. I take the time to change mine and get food packed in two satchels. Nothing fancy, just slices of bread and dried apples.

Clotho comes out, and I hand her the satchel. She takes it and belts it around her waist.

"I want you to leave first. Maximus will go with you. Take this dagger too."

She protests. "No, you need him with you."

She hands me back the dagger, and I am perplexed.

“I am a seasoned warrior. I’ll be fine. Please take him with you and the blade too,” I beg.

“I can’t. You are mortal, my love. Plus, it’s only a few hours of being apart.” She reassures me, but I am not convinced. I halfheartedly agree, but little does she know that her denial of his company won’t matter. He obeys me and will seek her out once she leaves. Clotho leaves before I do. We kiss, hug, and hold each other. Time feels warped as I pick her up. There is no time, but I wish I could have all of her for much longer. Seconds seem like hours, but the moment we part, it doesn’t feel like enough.

Our fingers brush once more before she starts down the road. I rush to her one more time and kiss her hard, wrapping my hands around her hips and pulling her in. “Be safe, my love.”

“You must do the same,” she whispers before our lips meet again.

I struggle to let her go this time, and I can see the turmoil rising in her expression.

I murmur close to her ear, “We will see each other soon enough and not be separated again.”

“I know,” she replies. “We can do this.”

"Yes, we can."

I finally relent and let her go. This is one of the hardest things I have done to date, watching her head down the road, not knowing what will happen to her. Part of me wants to rush off and say damn it all, we travel together, but I see the wisdom of her traveling alone after Iaso mentioning Zeus being able to track her godsaura. I gather there is a deity out there who can find the others. I didn't ask for clarification, but the power of the gods seems endless.

I tend to the farm one last time, then ask Phoebe and Alexius to watch things for me. Upon seeing me, they express surprise. "Where is Clotho?" Phoebe asks.

"She is waiting for me at the farm. We leave soon, and I need some help. Would you be able to ensure that all the animals are fed? Whatever you harvest from the fields is also yours to keep, as I am not sure when we will return."

"Is something the matter?" Phoebe's brows knit.

"Nothing right now, but there is some business to take care of. I promise she is safe."

"And you?" Phoebe asks, a subtle frown creases her forehead with worry.

"I will be safe too," I assure her.

Alexius remains silent and gives me a curt nod. He is not a man of many words, but a man of action. He ushers Phoebe back into their house. "You can trust that everything is in excellent hands." He says, "Phoebe worries too much. I know you have the skills to protect yourself."

"Aye. Thank you."

"Now go. I can sense you need to get going."

"Thank you again."

He reaches for my hand and gives it a firm shake. "You would do the same, old friend."

I bob my head in agreement. We've been through much as brothers of war, and I couldn't ask for better neighbors. Truly, they are family, and I am lucky they have my back.

I offer him a large sack of gold before making my way back home. Alexius fights it at first but takes it. He knows I will sneak that gold into his pockets. I make my way to the road praying silently to Ares, my patron god. I hope he answers and gives me the means to bring the fight to Zeus and not lose.

13

Fear That Eats

Clotho

Marcellus sends me on my way. I do not wish to bring attention to myself, so I travel on foot. The dim sunlight provides barely enough light to see where I am headed. But I prefer the cover of darkness to a bright, sunny day. I will need to glamor my face soon when dawn fully comes.

My path is tucked in between the trees near the road, as it is the fastest route to the Underworld. The cover of thickets and brush will keep me from being seen. I do not wish to venture deep into the woods here on Aetheria. I told Marcellus the same. Most mortals are unaware that the path to Hades is often in plain sight, not the less traveled thoroughfares like they often assume.

Hours pass, and the first bits of daylight are but a hint in the dark sky. I have sensed the presence of some being following me for some time now. They never show themselves but are close enough to not lose me. I know they mean no harm, so I pretend to be unaware. Soon enough, there is a second being trailing me. This time, the energy is distinct—dangerous. The hairs on my neck prick up, and I know the steps I take are not safe and part of me regrets not accepting the dagger Marcellus told me to take.

I keep myself alert, listening for anything that will give me information on who or what is following me. The crunch of footsteps on the forest floor fills my ears, and a wash of dread comes over me. They draw nearer, and I know whose energy creeps closer to my own.

Out of the shadows of thick trees in front of me, Minos steps out, his towering frame overshadowing me even with five feet of distance between us. "Clotho, is that you? What are you doing here?" His voice cracks with a sly tone.

I smile and direct my attention to him. He is a beast of a man. His facial features much like his father, Zeus:

chiseled angular chin and high cheekbones, golden locks cropped close to his ears, by all rights he is handsome, but his sky-blue eyes hold a certain cruelty, a darkness I cannot accurately describe with words. I answer his question right away. "Traveling the mortal world for all its beauty. Why did you follow me in silence for so long?" I speak, keeping my tone even so I don't reveal any of my emotions to this vicious demi-god.

"I had to be sure it was you. I hope you know my father is looking for you. Your sisters are too."

I feign surprise. "They are? I am well ahead of schedule on life threads. I needed a respite from such weary work. Spinning day in and day out is no simple task." I shrug.

"Without telling your sisters where you were going?" he asks, crossing his arms over his chest. Minos's brow knits up, and he takes a step closer.

I back up, knowing the cruelty that lies deep beneath his angelic features. "My sisters are not my keepers. I am not a child who needs to be tended to."

He edges closer, and an icy chill reverberates down my spine. Zeus has sent his cruelest son to collect me.

Has Pythia betrayed her oaths and my trust? Or did my sisters tell him I was close to Arcadia because they had no other choice?

"Why are you here?" I ask.

"You know why. He wants you back home on the Mounts."

My chances against Minos are slim, but not none. I dig my foot back and forth in the soil beneath me. My head bobs up and down, like I'm agreeing to such a foolish request. Zeus has no power over me, and he knows it, yet he will exert his efforts to show his authority. I answer to Hades and no one else.

I study Minos, every single shift in each muscle as he looms in front of me. "I am glad to see you are not resisting," he says. "I hope you are prepared to tell Zeus everything. You might as well come clean with me now."

"I have told you why. No hidden agenda. You should try being a Fate sometime." I see where this is going, and I will not entertain Minos further. I take a step closer to keep up my ruse. He seems to be confident that I won't put up a fight and lets down his guard, his shoulders relaxing.

I see the opportunity presented before me and pretend to adjust the ornate bracelet on my wrist. With a flick, I send it flying off down to the ground below. "Oh, no! My mother's bracelet!" I cry in mock distress.

As I bend over to retrieve it, I scoop up a handful of dirt in my free hand and toss it into Minos's eyes. He roars, clawing at his face. I take my chance and scramble away, breaking into a sprint. His howls of rage echo closely behind me.

I pick up my speed, but my escape is short-lived. Minos barrels into me from behind, tackling me to the ground. He pins me there, his crazed laughter echoing through the trees.

But a low snarl disturbs the air. A massive gray dog flashes out from the undergrowth in blurred fury. It's Maximus! He lunges forward and takes Minos's leg into his powerful jaws, tearing muscle from bone. This time, Minos's howls are filled with pain, and he quickly releases me to swat at the hound.

I roll away and gain my feet once more. "Maximus, come!" I call out.

He drops his prize and obeys me without fail, trotting to my side, very pleased with himself.

"Let's go," I tell him.

He wags his tail at me but turns to our enemy once more, a low growl emanating from deep in his chest.

I don't wait for Minos to react; I run, and Maximus follows. Through clenched teeth, Minos spits curses after us. "Craven witch! You and your mangy cur will pay for this treachery!" His rage-filled shrieks ricochet through the thick of the trees.

We escape the screams of agony and Minos's malevolent clutches, but I know we will not meet true safety until we arrive at the River Styx. Nothing else matters. We run for what seems like an hour nonstop toward our destination. The sun is now peeking over the horizon, and I must put on my disguise.

I stop, and Maximus halts right next to me. "I need to change my face, boy. Don't be alarmed. I will transform into an old woman, but it is still me."

He barks enthusiastically and sits on his haunches, waiting for me to do what needs to be done. I rub my palms together and silver light sparks between them. I cover my face and utter ancient tongues long forgotten.

"Gérontos eídōlon ep'emoi kalýptō." The words spill from my lips with such power the winds shift. As I remove my hands, the silver spark in my palms travels from the top of my head and across my face; violet gray strands replace my golden blonde hair, supple skin morphs into creases and discolored patches of flesh. Maximus tilts his head to one side quizzically, eyes bright and alert. Even his ears perk up at attention. He tips forward ever so slightly on his front paws, taking in the details of the magic I've worked.

"There, it is done," I say to Maximus, my voice now croaky and cracked. He sniffs at my hands curiously as the last bits of magic fade away.

Shaking out my new locks, I straighten to my full, diminutive height. "Let's get out of here, boy."

Maximus barks his agreement, and we head back out, keeping a steady pace through the woods despite the aged disguise I wear.

The sun rises higher, its weak rays struggling to penetrate the dense forest canopy. I let Maximus lead as he relies on more than sight alone. He will smell danger before I see it coming. While I would like to scold Marcellus for sending his faithful friend to guard me, I am forever grateful for his disregard of my request.

Zeus must have it out for me. I hope we do not cross paths with Minos again. He may be a demi-god, but there is a strength in him I have not encountered before. But maybe I am well protected ... after all, Maximus did more damage than I could. My thoughts turn to Marcellus, and I wonder if he is safe. I hope when he meets Kharon that the guardian of Styx will let him pass.

But for now, escaping Minos remains my top priority. I won't be any help if I am captured, and while I trust Kharon and Hades, I would prefer to make them aware of this whole situation before Minos comes barreling in.

I keep my sights forward on the path ahead, and I dare not look back. I focus on moving toward safety.

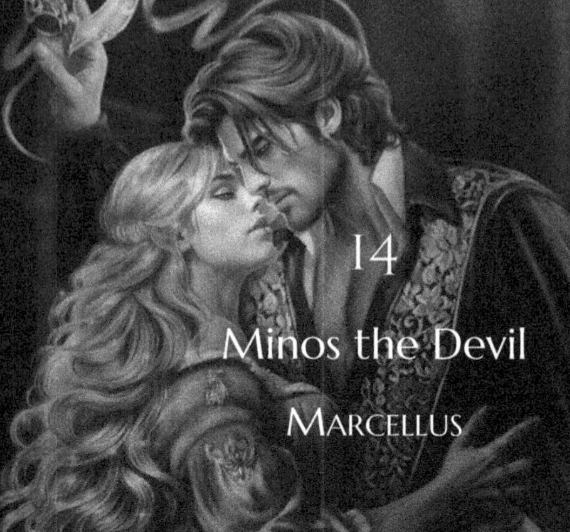

14

Minos the Devil

Marcellus

Clotho asked me to wait a couple of hours before traveling, but my gut tells me I need to head out now. I bid Phoebe and Alexius farewell—I know my farm is in excellent hands. I thank them for their help and hospitality, but lingering any longer goes against my instincts. Something is stirring in these lands, and I fear the worst. Hopefully, Clotho and Maximus are safe.

Grabbing my pack, I strike out into the woods, skirting the farm. The trees soon envelop me in cool shade, birdsong my only companion on the path that lies ahead. My senses are alive, taking in every detail. The slightest crack of twigs and an unfamiliar scent on the breeze catch my attention. My gut becomes heavy with unease.

Before long, I emerge onto the well-worn dirt road that guides me out of my country, Roma, and into Grecia. Hoofprints and wheel ruts testify to frequent traffic. I pull my hood up and blend in with the traveling merchants heading to New Athens.

Time passes unmarked as I plunge deeper into unfamiliar territory. Instead of heading south, I keep moving west, staying on the northern end of our continent. Once the travel way is free of people, I dart into the thickness of the trees.

The underbrush in this area is heavy and dense with red berries. There are probably bears feasting in preparation for winter. I slow down, ever mindful of my surroundings. The woods grow thicker, more tangled with each step. I decide to travel inward in search of a clearing, but a glint of metal up ahead catches my eye.

Drawing near, caution in my step, I uncover the gruesome sight of scattered weapons and supplies. Among the objects lay the torn remnants of men. Scavengers have already been at work here. I search in vain for clues to the identities of the bodies, but it seems these travelers, most likely merchants, were met with ambush and slaughter without a shred of mercy. Crouching low, I spot fresh tracks leading away, deep into the trees. My instincts tingle. Is the threat still nearby?

I begin tracking, determined to keep myself a step ahead of whomever or whatever committed such heinous acts. I wonder if it is lowly bandits, but spot giant lion-like prints on the ground along with large boot prints. Either way, traveling safely to the Underworld doesn't appear to be an option anymore.

I grab leaves and dirt, rubbing them on my arms and legs, and take a second to roll around on the ground to cover my scent. Rumors of a Chimera feasting on human flesh deep in the wood have spread through the markets over the years. I thought it was merely fiction, but the way those bodies were torn to shreds tells a different story.

Dread sits in my belly as I creep through the brush, staying low until I know the way forward is free from obstacles. I search for clues that may tell me if Clotho and Max came this way. I remind myself she is a goddess, but I worry anyway, especially knowing that she's still healing from the stab wound inflicted a month ago.

I am almost to another clearing when the moans of an injured man fill my ears. Maybe this is a merchant who can shed some light on the events I stumbled across. He is lying there, his leg bleeding all over the place.

I stand up and bid him a hello. "Hey there, let me help you," I say, crouching down to his level, but when he looks up, there is a familiarity in his face. This man is *Minos the Devil.* A cruel hearted sort, said to be the spawn of a god—and not just any god but Zeus.

I pretend not to recognize him and ask him if a Chimera attacked him. He shakes his head. "No, the bounty I chase had a Molossus in her company."

"A female bounty? That is something you don't hear every day," I say.

"This one has caused some trouble for our Olympians. I've been tasked with bringing her in."

"I see," I say, pausing a moment while wrapping his leg. "I wish you luck on your hunt." I'm lying, but at least I now know what Clotho and Maximus have been up to.

He eyes me suspiciously. "What is your name, good sir? Do you often help strangers in the woods?"

"Marcus. I helped the doctors on the battlefield in the last war, so by oaths taken, I have sworn to help those in need. And you are?"

"Ah, a man that doesn't recognize my face. I am Minos."

I pretend to be shocked and stop what I am doing. He chuckles. "I thought I'd get such response."

Good, my plan is working. He has no idea who I am, but I can't stay in his company for too long. "Do you need help getting to the road? I am sure any trader coming through would offer you a ride to the closest town nearby."

"No, I think I have it from here. All I need is a little more time to heal." He sniffs the air, and his eyes narrow. "You have their scent on you!" Minos's face turns fierce red with anger, and I pull away.

"I am not sure what you mean?" I continue to play dumb for the sake of not tangling with a demi-god.

"You smell like that damned hound who ripped my leg apart, too."

"I have no hound, sir. As you can see, I am alone. I am sure you are just smelling their scent in this space and nothing more," I try to convince him, and for a split second, he takes the bait, giving me time to spring to my feet.

Minos eyes me suspiciously but nods slowly. "You may be right, wanderer. The forest plays tricks on many."

I turn to leave, but his grip locks around my ankle with impossible strength, pulling me down. "But I am no true human, Marcus, if that's even your name. And I know her energy when it's imbedded deep in something or someone."

Minos takes hold of my ankle and pulls me down. We grapple on the forest floor, Minos snarling with fury. His leg wound bleeds through the bandage, but the fight seems to invigorate rather than weaken him. Remembering tales of his monstrous strength, I desperately make a play at his leg. My fingers find the torn flesh on his calf, and I dig in deep, twisting with brute force, hoping for the best. He howls, and his hold slacks enough that I wrench free and sprint as fast as my feet will carry me.

Behind me, Minos's screams echo through the trees. "Damn you! I will feast on your entrails, dog!"

I risk a glance back and see his thumb and index finger in his mouth. A loud whistled tune comes out, and the sky darkens with gray clouds that congeal to form the vague shape of a devilish head with twisted horns swirling up into dissipation. Lightning shoots across the sky and thunder cracks, and where it strikes, a monstrous beast emerges—a Chimera.

My heart sinks at the sight. There is no opposing such a force. All I can do is run. I dart through the dense thicket as the Chimera's melodic roar announces its hunt. I dare not look back again, instead focusing on evading its ravenous, hungry jaws for as long as Fate allows.

15
Tricking the Devil
Marcellus

The hot breath of the Chimera burns against my back as I race through maze-like tree trunks that impede me. I search for a clearing to gain the second needed for a miraculous escape.

Minos' maniacal laughter echoes all around me, taunting me with words that pierce my heart. "I'll let the Chimera handle you while I deal with that wretched Moira, but they won't kill you. No. I will make you watch as I torture Clotho and take her as my own. I'll give you the dissatisfaction of watching me penetrate her. Over and over until she moans my name willingly. I will show her why humans are inferior to those with Olympia in their blood."

My blood boils, and rage builds up inside me. He. Will. Not. Touch. Her. I grit my teeth and focus on one goal: keeping Minos distracted so that he doesn't catch up to her. But the Chimera is relentless in its pursuit, its serpent tail striking out at me with each turn.

The hiss and slither of its tongue grazes my ear, but I swerve left, upping my speed. I swear I hear Clotho's voice calling out to me, urging me to keep going. With renewed determination, I push past the pain and exhaustion, knowing that love will see me through to the end.

The beast is twice the size of any bear I've encountered, but its size doesn't stop me from using its own weight against it. I ram into Minos, causing him to stumble and collide with his loyal pet. It turns fiercely to protect its master, but I am behind it, my dagger drawn from its hiding place. I slash the hindquarters of the monster, and it wails in agony.

I leap over the creature and land on Minos, dagger to his neck. "You will not touch her as long as I live." I have mere seconds, and I'll do whatever it takes to ensure my love reaches the Underworld safely. I drag my blade across his neck. His eyes widen and he stares up at me in raw panic. I roll off when that hot breath meets my neck again. The Chimera yowls for its master and claws at me but stays near Minos.

A wretched, bubbling sound rises from his throat as he stands despite the injury I've inflicted upon him. His hands fly to his neck, stanching the flow of ichor that passes for his blood. The beast licks at Minos's flesh and throws back its head with a roar.

I stare in awe, alarm filling my gut as the wound knits itself closed before my eyes.

I scramble backward in horror. Any hope of defeating such a monster is now dashed. Minos smiles cruelly at me and reaches out to seize my throat, but the Chimera snarls and snaps, not wanting to share its prey with its master.

Minos barks a command, and it withdraws reluctantly. "Run, pathetic human—dash away like a meek rabbit to its warren. I'll be along shortly to tear it down, suffocating you in its depths."

I waste no time complying. Only a fool would stay planted where they stand. I flee into the forest, satisfied with my endeavor. His attention is solely on me now. I've unleashed his full wrath upon me. *Good, this will give Clotho the time she needs to appeal to Hades.*

I weave in a zig-zag pattern through the wood. The trees part ahead and reveal a sheer cliff face. My feet meet the edge as I peer down below. A low roar fills my ears as the waves crash on the rocks below. Behind me comes the crashing of undergrowth as my pursuers close in for the kill.

With no other choice, I scream, “Ares! I plead with you now. Help me!” I take a flying leap, barreling down at full speed into the deep, blue darkness of a turbulent sea.

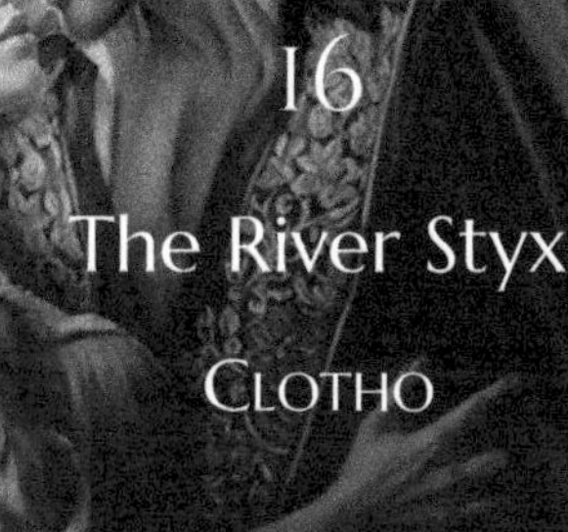

16

The River Styx

Clotho

There is something happening behind Maximus and me, but I dare not venture on paths we've already traversed. The only thing I know for sure is that Minos is still hot on our trail. His nose is like a bloodhound's. Once he catches a scent, he will not lose it, and he never gives up on finding his target.

Maximus pauses, his ears pivoting back and forth. He senses something else we both yearn for—the presence of Marcellus. A surge of tightness seizes over my heart, constricting it in a vise-like grip. Does this mean he is nearby? What if Marcellus tangles with Minos next? No mortal has ever survived Minos in combat, but my thread, which intertwines with Marcellus's, should protect him. Yet worry still permeates

my entire being, and I find it increasingly hard to tame the disquiet seizing my mind.

Deep down, I sense my love still lives. But dread continues to lash through me. So, I focus on the only thing that I can—hoping that this horrible feeling in my gut is nothing but a trick. For now, all I can do is push forward with Maximus. I must rely on my intuition that Marcellus is okay. I cling to this, using it to fuel my resolve even against the grimmest of odds.

I cannot believe Zeus sent his most depraved spawn after us. Not only this, but Minos is only half-god. I know he meant it as an insult. I am a lowly Moira in his eyes. And sending Minos is his way of saying just how low he thinks my position really is.

The whole thing makes my blood boil. My great-grandmother spun Zeus's thread. Even he cannot escape the Fates, but many often misunderstand those who deal with Death. Even the gods on the Mounts are clueless. I breathe in. My steps take me closer and closer to Hades' domain. Soon, I will be with those who cherish me, and I can't wait to see Kharon. We've always been friends since our births. I've been on the Mounts for too long and visiting him is quite overdue. If only it were under different circumstances.

I make my way into a dense thicket of trees, where all the light is swallowed whole by their closeness. Maximus pads faithfully at my side, hackles raised as the energy around us shifts. He, too, senses the shivery resonance penetrating our surroundings, which means we are almost at our destination. As we delve further into the shadowed boughs, the mossy veil draped over many low branches tickles the top of my head as I pass.

I place my hand on a pitted stone, feeling the otherworldly forces swirling beyond a permeable barrier. We are so close to the entryway to the Underworld. Passing through the natural curtain, I behold a river flowing inside a darkened cave in front of me. Overgrown honeysuckle vines hang near the entrance and spread out into a wild orchard of pomegranate trees dappling the outer banks of the stream.

My pace slows. There are eyes watching us from the trees. "Make yourself known. Are you friend or are you foe?" I ask.

Persephone steps out from the trees in a powdery blue gown that moves with the breeze even though she stands still now. Raven locks frame her face. Creamy white streaks peek out from the darker layers that hug her shoulders. And a delicate dusting of shadowy charcoal accentuates her high cheekbones, adding depth to her ethereal beauty—as lady of spring and queen of the Underworld. A shimmering obsidian crown rests on her head, contrasting her dual-hued eyes and pale skin. One is a deep blue and the other a rich amethyst. All her loveliness reflects her dual dominion over the cyclical dances that are life and death.

"My Lady." I bow.

"Stand, my dearest Clotho. I know why you've come, and I fear that the first test is already upon you and your love. I have never seen the god-king so angry."

I choke up and nod my head. Minos is the test. A cruel and unwarranted one, but Zeus is ruthless when he thinks he's been slighted. If he'd realize that the love I have with Marcellus has nothing to do with our immortal status, things would be different.

Persephone senses my discontent. “You know the rules: no mortal and immortal shall be together. Especially if the love inhibits or impacts the immortal’s ability to do their job. You did something that altered the fibers of this world. Zeus had Pythia discern what, and he’s decreed all of Aetheria will be a test of your love. Prove to him you still have the best interests of this world in your heart, and he may let the man you love live.”

“Did he tell you and Hades what I have done?” I ask.

“Yes.”

“Then what are your thoughts?”

“I understand why you did what you did.” Persephone reaches out and takes my hand, squeezing it gently.

“What comes next?”

“I want you to know if Marcellus makes it to Kharon, we will grant him sanctuary and Minos will retreat.”

“If you both knew everything, why did you not come to me sooner? Are you saying Minos trails Marcellus instead of me?” I ask, my anger flaring.

"Because, you know as well as I do, you must prove yourselves and your love. Set things right. Your power unleashed Cronos from the realm of Tartarus. And Zeus also thinks your love is merely a childish infatuation. I'm sorry, but there is no other way. If Zeus wants to put you to the test, he can and he will. He is the god of this world. We are always under his rule. I cannot say he always makes sense but take this kindness for what it is. And yes, Minos has locked his sights on your human. The next test is more grueling. Cronos will not be as kind as Minos. You must choose now. Will you face Cronos alone in a bid to spare your mortal lover's life?"

I don't know why she asks when she knows my answer. "I'll go."

Persephone approaches, embraces me in a deep hug, and whispers, "Show those tired Olympians what we are made of. Much like my love story, yours is worth the battle to come. My energies and your sisters' are with you now. Go to the River Styx and have Kharon help you to the next portal, where you'll find Cronos waiting. I hope for your sake he is amiable since you are the daughter of Nyx." She squeezes my hand. "Are you taking the hound?" she asks, looking at my companion.

"I don't know. Maximus. You can go find Marcellus. I am fine to proceed to the next test alone."

He growls low in his belly and nudges my arm as if to say *no, I am staying*.

"Okay, we stay together then?" I ask, and he barks enthusiastically.

Persephone snaps her fingers, and Cerberus appears. "I cannot help you with defeating Cronos, proud warrior dog, but Cerberus certainly can. Don't dally long. Kharon's patience is thin today."

Kharon is my best friend. I doubt he'll be disappointed to see me, but I often forget that others aren't aware of the bond we share. I am sure, considering all things, he will still be happy to see me.

She fades off behind the trees, plucking a ripened fruit from the branches, her words filling my ears. "Don't forget to feast on the seeds of the fruit of Hades. This area is blessed beyond measure. A gift from him in your time of need."

I scoff. The idea of a fruit being helpful makes me angry, and I don't know why. Hades and Persephone are powerful, but doubt boils to the brim inside me. I expected more help than this. What can the guardian of the Underworld and fruit accomplish?

Cerberus towers six feet over me. His three enormous wolf-like heads drip with slobber. Maximus and he play like puppies while I stare at my feet. This is the help offered to defeat a Titan. Persephone and Hades must have extreme faith in my abilities. I am not too sure myself. The Moirai were never permitted to view their own threads. What happens next remains to be seen.

If Hades and the other upper gods know what I did, are they also aware of a mortal's blade injuring me? I worry my strength is not at its peak. I pluck several pomegranates from the trees and begin feasting. Maybe this is the purpose of me eating the fruit of the Underworld?

Still displeased with the assistance given, I mumble to myself that not even my family or truest friend Kharon share the level of love Marcellus has for me. Granted, I know the love is different, but I know where I'd stand if they were in my place. I would be with them, willingly supporting their right to love whom they love. I'd fight alongside them. Instead, I am to eat pomegranates and do my best to prove what I know is real to a bunch of tired and useless immortals who value their own hides above all else. Many threads I have spun, and humans, flawed and imperfect as they are, have shown time and again how selfless they can truly be.

Maybe eternal life has the gods and goddesses all jaded, but I'd like to believe there is still something more to live for. Something like the love I share with Marcellus.

Tired from eating pomegranate seeds, I sip the nectar from the honeysuckle instead. Cerberus is still here. There is some exchange of energies or words between the hound of Hades and Maximus. I wish I was privy to the exchange, but if Cerberus can ensure his safety, then I am glad for his help.

My mind wanders to Marcellus. I swear I had felt him nearby after we ran from Minos. I question if I should have turned around. If he tangles with that abomination, will he make it to Kharon? I must have faith like humans do. *Marcellus lives.* He said there were things owed. From what gods, I do not know. Cerberus and Maximus approach me and push me toward the entrance of the cave. I wince. Caves have not been on my favorite list for some time. Fleeting images of the oracle's cavern pierce my thoughts. I breathe in and release my anxiety, shuffling my feet forward.

I follow the river's winding bends and turns. The farther we travel inward, the more things change. The water, once a deep, muddied blue, is now glowing aquamarine. Ordinary gray and reddish-brown rocks have been replaced with glimmering crystal beds. Some of these untouched gems pulse with a glow that lights the path ahead. The river widens, and there, standing near a large ferry, is Kharon, hooded and cloaked. His gnarled hands hold his pole steady to the ground. A lantern sits upon carved stone, illuminating his sullen countenance further.

He blinks his golden eyes before setting his gaze upon me. "I wasn't expecting you, dear friend," he says, appearing to be puzzled that I am here.

"Interesting. Did no one tell you what is going on?" I ask.

"I am always left out of the loop. Their excuse is I am always ferrying souls. Which is wholly untrue."

"Let's see. Where to begin ... I fell for a human, changed his threads, and now Zeus wants him dead as far as I can tell. And I need your help." I don't hold back. Kharon is my oldest and closest friend outside the mounts. I can speak freely to him about everything that has transpired.

His jaw drops, his brow raising, the wrinkles on his forehead becoming more pronounced. "By the Styx! Tell me you're having me on? You cannot be serious. Did Hades put you up to this?" He chuckles but notes my unchanged and serious demeanor.

"No. This is not a farce. I need your help, old friend." I pause. "Please. When Marcellus arrives, grant him safe passage and keep Zeus's lackey, Minos, off him."

"You are serious. Minos the Devil? This is not ... optimal." Kharon fidgets with his pole nervously as the implications sink in.

“I know what I ask is a lot. I am sorry to put you in this position.”

He studies me for a few seconds, then approaches and softly rests my hand on the steady bend of his arm. “I am your confidant without question. I will always be there for you, no matter what. Where do I need to take you next?” he asks.

“Wherever Cronos is,” I reply.

“This is ... more severe than I thought. I will need to search him out. Give me a moment,” Kharon says.

I am fearful of what is coming, but there is no other choice. Confronting the Titan is inevitable for me. I hope he has more sense than our god-king does, but I, too, would want freedom from Tartarus. A hellish prison surrounded by the great sea of Poseidon. The escape he managed speaks volumes of his will—a will that I will soon face. No Fate who came before told me that combining threads would lead to this. Only that it would disrupt the natural order, and we should know better than to mess with such a thing.

Some part of me surely knew better. Maybe those before me had no clue what would happen? Maybe there were always variables? So it was best to leave it alone. But I did not. My choices have led me to this moment, and I will face one of the oldest gods of this world.

Titans are primitive gods, the first of our kind, and Cronos is mightier than Zeus. Truth is, he had his siblings to aid him after he forced their release. How will I beat such an opponent *alone*? Surely not with fruit seeds. While I am grateful for Persephone greeting me, I ask myself, where is Hades in all of this?

Kharon senses my unease. "There is turmoil boiling to the surface. You've gotten this far. You can go further. I hope you know this." He rests his hand on my shoulder, trying to comfort me.

"I feel little hope right now. I thought I'd see Hades, but only Persephone greeted me and bid me to eat pomegranates. Like it will solve all my problems." My shoulders slump in defeat, but Kharon's eyes gleam with ancient wisdom. I meet his gaze, puzzled by it.

"Do not dismiss the simplest of magics. They are more powerful than you can imagine," he reassures me. "And you are not alone. This old ferryman will stand at your side, as will others."

"You make it sound so simple, like I didn't inadvertently let loose a Titan into this world. I have changed Fate. I have played with a destiny that is not mine. There are consequences not yet revealed. Will you still stand with me when my sisters are next? Facing perilous danger? We may be a thousand years old, but those two have kept such innocence. Innocence I cannot let be destroyed. The Moirai will never be the same because of my actions. I combined my thread with a human's." I blurt it out for Kharon and all the souls close to hear.

His shoulders rise and fall with a heavy sigh. "I've ferried souls for eons, but this ... this takes the proverbial Tartarus cake, my dear. Hmm, we could do with some right now. Even just a slice."

I chuckle a bit as Kharon mutters about cake. He has one thing right. No one can top the cakes from Tartarus. Especially the ones my mother Nyx makes.

He glances over, but I can't bear to look my friend in the eye, turning my concentration to the pebbled floor of the cave instead. "Now you know why fear sits with me," I mumble, digging my boots in between the loose stones.

"Aye, but I am still asking you to trust our Lady. And our Lord, too. Zeus is a baby playing at the game of king. Hades is *king*, and never forget it. You are a master of the weaves of Fate, of life itself. Do not let a pompous ass like Zeus shrink your power."

"You say this even after I've told you what I've done?" I ask.

"You love the man? What wouldn't a person, god or otherwise, do for *true love*?" With a gentle motion, Kharon raises my chin to meet his gaze. "Dearest and oldest friend. I am not here to judge you on past actions. I am here to see what you do next. While your intentions were good, unforeseen consequences are now yours to deal with. Use your wisdom and love to mend this, and all will be well."

"That is a lot of faith in a Moira that knew—*knows better*—but still I did what I did."

"Do you regret it?" he asks.

"No, I'd do it again as long as Marcellus lives."

"Then you don't need me to tell you otherwise. Ready yourself, and I'll take you to Cronos. Spark a deal with the old god. He is not as unreasonable as Zeus would have you think." Kharon directs me to the edge of the water and helps me onto the ferry. Maximus follows suit, and Cerberus travels down the edge of the river up ahead.

My mind spins. I am not sure what he means by striking up a bargain with Cronos. What could a Titan want? Maybe Kharon knows more than he is letting on. So, I ask him, "What does Cronos want? That I could possibly deliver for his quiet return to prison?"

"So quick to ask the right questions. Good. He wants Tartarus to be his boon. A prison no more, but a home. Make Zeus give it to him."

"How do I do that? What an impossible task!" I shriek.

"Not impossible. I know you can converse with your brother and sisters through your minds alone. Bid them to seize and secure the one thing Zeus cannot control." He cracks a wicked smile and keeps his gaze on me.

My voice shakes. "You're not suggesting what I think you are?"

"Oh, but I am. Thanatos won't hesitate to fulfill your query. We know the sort of mischief he likes to get in, and this will top them all." His devilish grin widens as I consider what he's suggesting.

"If I do this, then I am truly mad."

"Aren't we all, when it comes to real love?" he replies.

I say nothing more and nod my head. I know what I must do next. I hope Kharon is right. I reach out into the nether and connect my mind to my brother's, with a single request and pure hope that he's up to the task.

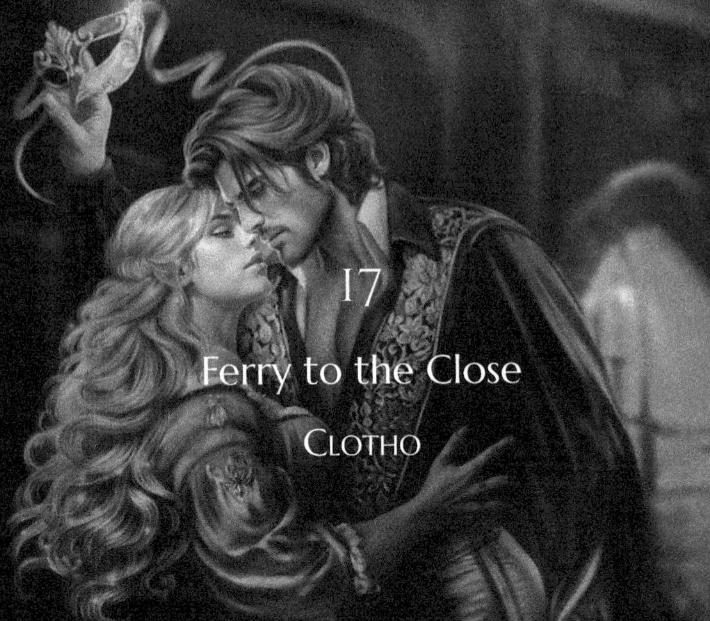

17

Ferry to the Close

Clotho

We travel further down the Styx for what seems like hours. Kharon focuses on guiding us through wending tunnels where any other soul would surely get lost. Smoky quartz clusters glimmer in the dull bluish light emitted from the river itself. My brother has given me his answer, and I feel hopeful for the first time since talking to Iaso.

Maximus lies curled up against my legs. I take this time to give him extra love and talk to him. "I am so glad you're here with me, boy. But I worry Marcellus will need you, too."

He grunts and nudges his muzzle into my hands. I hold his face and peer deep into his eyes. He doesn't seem worried at all. I sense he is ready for anything. I wonder if he misses Marcellus and what he is thinking

in that regard. Guilt threads its way through me. I must remember that Marcellus was a soldier in Roma. They value warriors and train hard. Ares himself stamped his thread box. I should have less anxiety over what Marcellus is capable of.

Even during our days on the farm, he spent time in the mornings training while he thought I slept. Visions of his hard-earned muscles fill my mind, and a warmth surges through me. Even when we're apart, he sets my soul ablaze.

Everyone so far has told me many are on my side. This means Marcellus also has them in case he needs help. My biggest struggle to date is having faith all will turn out right. I am constantly dealing out threads of life, seeing the beginning, middle, and end. Faith and hope are hard for me to accept.

Yet I must, for Marcellus and our future. Together. I want nothing more. I need no other boon besides his love. Not even death separates the bond our two souls create. Certainty must encompass all of me if I am to succeed.

Kharon slows the ferry. Our destination is ahead. My nerves threaten to swallow me whole. I know my plan and what I must do next, but will this Titan listen or rush to battle? Unknowns still haunt me around every corner. I am used to seeing things unfold, but a Fate may never spin their own thread. Another was responsible for my weave, and I am very curious. What did she see? Did she know? Why was my life left up to an oracle's warning?

I do not discount the power of prophecy, but the means by which it is delivered—always cloaked in riddles and half messages. I suppose this is to ensure free will. But in that same vein, I had more details than most ever receive. I knew of the chaos and ruin. Even now, deep in the Underworld, I sense the shift in mortal lands.

I knew I could stop this but chose not to.

I doubt I will witness all this mayhem firsthand, since I am facing the Titan responsible for its creation. But I am fearful of his time-manipulating power, as I am clueless of what will happen as I approach his location. Instead of caring about what he could do to me, I am holding on to the hope that my thread of immortality is enough to protect Marcellus while enduring Cronos's temporal alterations.

The ferry drifts around a bend, and a massive chasm splits the landscape ahead. Within the fissure, tendrils of energy writhe about. The colors of each tendril vary, creating a strange rainbow of distortions, most likely in the time-stream.

The ever-present shadows of the Underworld seem to recoil from this place, gathering thickly at the edges of the void. Even Cerberus lets out a whimper from where he trails beside the ferry.

"Cerberus, join us on the ferry," I say, but the great three-headed hound is full of apprehension.

Kharon turns to me. "He's always hated the ferry, but I agree once we enter the chasm, who knows what those threads of time will do to us? Come, boy, just this once, please."

Cerberus edges close to the ferry's side and climbs up in. It is quite a sight to see such a large beast shiver with fear. But I notice Maximus's fur is raised up on his back, too. They must be aware of something Kharon and I cannot sense, and that realization immediately sets me on edge.

Kharon's pole pulls us through the water, toward the chasm. My breath hitches as we descend into its depths. The ferry's nose plunges down rapidly. Wisps of energy whip through my hair as violets, reds, and oranges course around us in fury. The waters we travel shift speeds. One moment, we are traveling at a snail's pace; the next, our feet barely remain on the deck. I tiptoe to Kharon and take hold of his staff, which remains planted to the surface of his vessel.

"Hold on tight!" he roars as we fly down the vertical waters. Both dogs huddle close, and I put one hand on Maximus.

The boat shifts once more and plops down into horizontal waters. Kharon takes care and peers into the abyss beyond us. "Beyond this point, time itself bends and twists under his touch," he rumbles. "Tread carefully, my dear."

Winds sigh eerily from the darkness in front of me. The gloom flickers with a hue of cyan and illuminates shards of other days and places. But they shift and warp beneath a strange tide of water floating just above them. Mountains rise and fall in seconds, civilizations living and dying in the blink of an eye.

Somewhere within, Cronos awaits. He could easily rend my life asunder with a single flick of his wrist. I steel myself, knowing my future with Marcellus now hangs in the balance. I must use all the power of the Fates for what comes next.

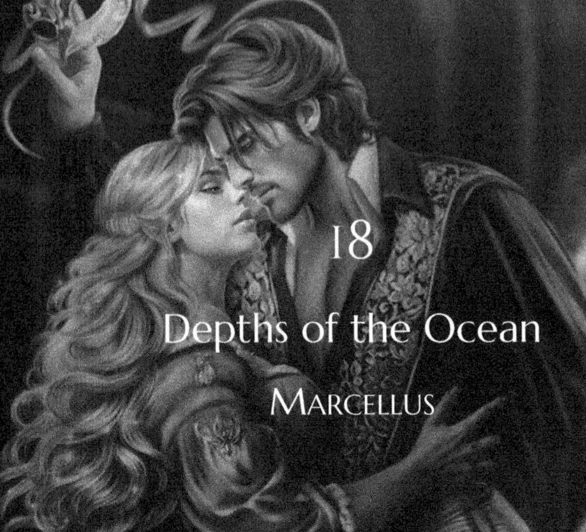

18

Depths of the Ocean

Marcellus

The sheer cliff face races by as I hurtle toward the vast, churning ocean below. The wind tears at my clothes and whips strands of hair into my eyes, obstructing my view. My heart races with fear as I think of Clotho, wishing for a way out of this dire situation. A way out where I find her in my arms once more.

I pray to every god I can think of, desperate for their aid. The water rushes up to meet me, the impact forcing all the air from my lungs. Saltwater floods my mouth and stings my eyes as I am dragged under the thrashing waves. The force is almost too much to bear, and darkness threatens to swallow me whole.

But then, I feel gentle arms wrapping around me. Lifting me up to the surface and carrying me through the tide. Through blurry vision, I make out two figures on either side of me. As my sight clears, I see they are nereids—daughters of Poseidon himself.

One speaks in a voice so melodic it could lull me to sleep. "Poseidon's daughters come to assist you on the next leg of your journey."

As we travel toward the shore, my body feels weak and heavy from the struggle against the sea. The other nereid turns to me and says, "Ares himself has deemed you worthy. In response to his call, our lord sent us to help you."

A new surge of strength floods my waterlogged body. Finally, my patron god answers my pleas for help. I thought he had abandoned me in my greatest time of need, but he hasn't, and to have Poseidon's support as well ... I am speechless.

The first nereid speaks. "He never abandoned you, but Zeus has trapped him on the mounts."

Before I can speak, a deafening roar splits through the air. Minos and the Chimera are still in hot pursuit. There is no time to waste. The nereids quicken their speed. I strain my neck to look behind us and see that our pursuers are closing in at an alarming pace. Minos's furious screams blend with the Chimeras monstrous snarls, creating a cacophony of unholy rage that shakes me to my core. I may have gotten the upper hand earlier, but it never guaranteed safe passage to the Underworld. No, it was merely a way to keep me several steps ahead.

The nereids' graceful movements slice through the water with lithe power. Their floating hair ripples out, undulating with each movement of the waves. Though they are hampered by my limp weight, their fair features remain set with steely resolve.

My new enemies loom alarmingly close as clouds spiral above, becoming thicker and darker by the second. It's as if Minos commands the very skies, much like his father. He bellows a challenge that sets the very winds upon us, pulling us back from our destination, dragging us under the current. But the nereids battle the torrents with all their strength.

We breach the surface long enough for me to choke gasps of air before the undertow drags us under again. Through swirling foam, I glimpse the Chimera's leering maw snapping at the tails of my allies, its fell breath poisoning the waters. The sisters throw caution to the wind, their luminous skin blurring into ethereal symbols as magic grants them newfound speed. Despite our best efforts, the monster persists, reaching out with its claws to snatch us from the depths.

Between thrashing swells and jagged rocks jutting out like sharp teeth, our only hope is a small isle's sandy beach. I copy the nereids' movements with my legs and push beyond all limits in a final sprint for life itself.

We race to the edge of land, the tail fins on my rescuers morphing into legs. Surging from the surf, we flee up the sand and plunge into the protective woodlands, where bushes, and bracken, mask our presence.

Amidst gasps for breath, one of my rescuers speaks up. "I am Amphinome," she says, her voice laced with urgency. "And this is my sister, Dyname." I notice they are identical twins, but while Amphinome's hair is a dark ebony, Dyname's is a striking vermilion, which is the only way for me to tell them apart.

The two speak in a language I am not familiar with. While they converse, I search for ways to cover our scents and hide from our enemies. I rub leaves and dirt on my arms.

"We need to blend in with the forest as best we can to escape Minos and the Chimera's clutches," I whisper.

Amphinome turns to me, her eyes locking onto mine. "The mortal is correct," she says. "We need to blend in with the trees before it's too late." Their incandescence fades to a dull shimmer.

Dyname nods in agreement. "We should not linger here," she adds. "We must take to the deep."

I know they are speaking about the ocean. "How?" I ask, feeling the weight of my human limitations.

"Fret not," Amphinome replies, a mischievous glint in her eye. "We have a gift to offer, unless you'd rather face Minos and his beast head-on?"

"What gift?" I ask cautiously, not wanting to agree to something without knowing what it entails.

"Smart mortal," Dyname remarks to her sister.

Amphinome smiles. "The gift of breathing underwater."

"A gift freely given?" I ask, hesitant to accept.

"Yes, there is no obligation on your end," she says.

"Why?" I'm curious why nothing is expected in return.

They reply in unison. "Clotho has been a loyal friend to us. That is reward enough. We'd like to repay her by helping the one she loves."

"Then I will accept this boon in the spirit that it is offered."

The sisters clutch my forearms, and an electric shock shoots through me. Searing pain races through my entire body and sparks one last time on the sides of my neck. A sharp cry escapes my lips, and I take a step back, watching a low light dash through my veins before disappearing.

"Now we are ready to travel to the other side of this island." Dyname grins.

I am speechless. My head nods forward in agreement and all three of us head out.

My thoughts go back to their words. I am curious about Clotho's past with the mention of her loyalty and friendship to the nereids. But my gut wrenches still. If I had known Minos would be a test, I wouldn't have let us be separated.

I also fear that she will encounter someone or something much stronger than the demigod. The thought of Clotho facing unknown dangers alone makes my chest constrict with dread. My heart hammers as we plunge into the forest ahead, the branches clawing like grasping hands propelled by my restless imagination.

What terrors might lurk in the woodland depths for a lone maiden? My pulse roars in my ears, drowning out the words the twins speak. Dark visions flood my sight. My mind conjures phantoms of leering satyrs and savage beasts, talons ripping that delicate skin I know so well.

I struggle to keep breathing through the panic rising in my throat. Each footfall that distances me from her feels like betrayal. I know she is immortal, but the wound weakened that part of her. I can only hope that more friends have come to her aid as well.

The nereids glide soundlessly before me, their aura of calm grace at odds with the turmoil in my head. Still, I push on, drawing strength from memories of Clotho's touch to weather each new fear. Whatever threats bar my path, her light is the lodestar guiding my way through swirling tides of dread and resolve. Only her sweet voice can still this pounding heart.

The roar of the Chimera breaks the peace hanging in the air. Minos and his beast are on land. The distant, muffled sound assures me they are far away, giving us an opportunity to escape. We make haste deeper into the trees. I am careful with each step I take, watching for fallen twigs and branches.

A part of me wishes I moved with the grace of the nereids. Amphinome stirs up the soil and leaves behind us, removing traces of the path we take. Minutes pass, but it feels like hours as we continue to weave between the trunks growing in numbers in front of us.

We hear a loud snap echo about, and the twins shove me into a hollowed tree. I watch as they both effortlessly climb two trees next to the one I hide in. The twins, despite being water creatures, blend into the leaves of the oaks they rest on. I can barely make out their eyes.

I rub dirt on my arms and press my body into the recesses of the tree and wait. I expect any minute now we will see Minos and the Chimera searching for us. Yet there is not a soul to be seen. I temper my breathing, drawing air softly through my nostrils and releasing it in near-silent exhalations. I hope to become one with the flora I am occupying—that I will not give away my position to the enemy if they are close to us now.

Minos storms into the small clearing, bellowing in his rage. Blood stains his clothes from his neck down to his waist. I can't help but smile at my handiwork. The Chimera's hellish form crashes into him soon after, sniffing the air and snarling.

In the neighboring boughs, I see fear filling up tiny irises. Yet, Amphinome and Dyname manage to keep deathly still, magic veiling their scent as the beast comes dangerously close to each of them.

Time drags at a snail's pace as the hellhounds quarter the forest floor. Each snapped twig sends my heart into my throat. I remain still. Much of this depends on me keeping my composure. I do not have magic to lend me a hand like they do.

At last, the beasts' frustrated vociferations fade into the distance. Just as tense muscles unwind, I hear the soft pattering of feet on the ground. Nymphs emerge from the brush, glancing about with sly smiles on angelic faces.

One speaks low in tone. "All is clear. You can come out now."

The twins appear first and leap down, embracing the nymph at the center of the group. I am not sure what type she is as there is a stream next to us. Dyname squeaks, "Carya, what a pleasant surprise. I thought for sure you'd keep yourselves well hidden."

Carya takes the twins by the arms and takes a stride in my direction. "We could not help but overhear you are assisting Clotho and her human?"

It seems every immortal is aware of our situation. Lead sits in my gut. Not all these beings are friends. Will these nymphs prove to be friend or foe? I cannot tell.

"Yes, we are escorting her lover to safety." Dyname gives the information freely, but Amphinome watches with concern in her eyes. I don't blame her.

"Do you need sanctuary with the Dryads of Kasos this eve? You can tell the human to come out of his hiding place now." Carya beckons toward me like she knew where I was all along.

I emerge from the hollow, planting my feet beneath me with care. "A kind offer to a mortal, but the night wears on, and I must find my way back to the path that leads me to where I need to go." I offer a slight bow, being mindful not to offend.

Carya's eyes gleam knowingly, unsettling in their perceptiveness. It seems that Dyname is too trusting, whereas her sister is clearly more cautious. I share the same sentiment. These nymphs may wish us well, but I remain wary of ulterior motives.

"Come, cousins, at least join us for a bit of rest and sustenance?" Carya begs.

"Oh, please, please." Dyname's eyes light up.

I watch Amphinome. She smiles slightly and glances in my direction. My mortal status requires the two things they offer. I know this. She does, too. She nods slowly and accepts. "We will. I look forward to your hospitality. It's been ages since our last sojourn."

Carya asks, "To where do you travel so late, while Minos's fury blackens the skies?" As she speaks, her gaze flickers to the shadowed trees, subtly directing our path. Dyname chatters blithely away about our situation, oblivious to the undercurrents her elder sister heeds.

Amphinome moves closer to me, and Carya smiles then says, “I promise the human is safe while in our company.”

Amphinome listens keenly, her magic readied beneath nimble glowing fingers.

“Rest for a few hours and we will lead you all to the edges of the island without running into Minos or his beast once more,” Carya speaks, her voice carrying a melodic tune that draws me in, but I still want to say no.

Carya looks at Amphinome and then at me. Dyname still none-the-wiser about what is transpiring. She tilts her head. “I promise you will be safe and free of any harassment in our sacred wood. Just follow me and see. The dryads here will obey me and leave the human alone, I swear.”

There it is again. Something so sweet and alluring in her voice, how could I say no? I shift my sights to Amphinome, who still seems apprehensive, but she nods slowly, as if to say I can accept. While I still hold some doubts, I am inclined to accept what protections these beings offer. We need the reprieve, so I shake my head as Carya’s gaze remains on me.

"Your shelter we'll gladly take until we are ready to continue forward. Thank you, kind lady of the wood." I bow.

She reaches out to take my hand, but I pull away. Her painted lips thin, but she turns, beckoning us into the deepening green. I follow, wondering where they will take us. Stories of the hidden groves on Kasos are spread far and wide on Aetheria. So are the tales of nymphs' seductions. I only hope they are the friends they claim to be and do not tempt me. I am leery of Carya's promise going in, but I do not have the energy to face those who hunt me right now.

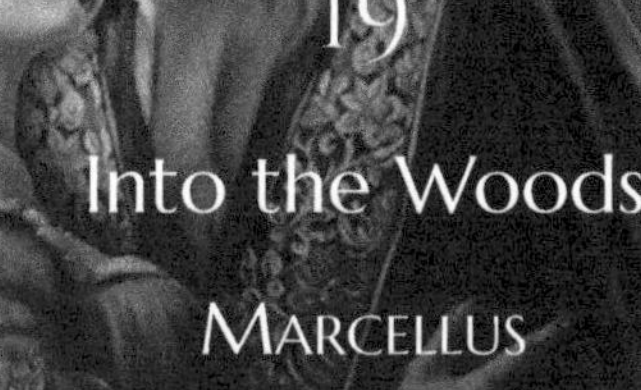

19

Into the Woods

Marcellus

The darkness of the forest engulfs us with each footstep we take. Carya leads us further into the gloom. Off in the distance, the howl of the Chimera sets my entire being on edge. I never want to tangle with that beast again if I can help it. Minos is relentless in his pursuit. I know part of his determination to find me is my own doing. I have slighted him more than most mortal men, and I escaped his grasp.

Moss and flowering vines part, revealing a bright moonlit glade. Dryads flit between the trees. Our group is greeted warmly, yet Carya's calculating eyes linger on me as she leads us in. Her gaze causes me great discomfort. I brush it off with a smile in her direction and a slight bow.

Rest is wanted and necessary. I'd be a fool not to take this chance. I do not know what lies ahead after this. As we proceed inward to the center of the glade, there are tables of food and drink laid out invitingly. Carya directs us to empty seats. I partake sparingly while Dyname indulges without care, but Amphinome samples little bites as well, scanning the dryads gathering at each table. I take heed and keep my own senses as sharp as this place will allow.

Carya comes up to me and offers me a chalice of wine. I hold the cup in my hands at first but set it down. Her face darkens and I take another bite of the vegetables on my plate as she stares me down.

Carya's fingers touch the cup, and she plops it right in front of me. "You should taste the wine here. It is the best in all Aetheria."

"I fear the dullness of the mind that comes with the drink. I need my senses about me as much as everyone here. Minos will not stop until he finds a way in and, trust me, he will."

"You doubt our powers, mortal?"

"No, but you should fear the lengths Minos will go to in order to finish the hunt he is on," I warn.

"I see." Carya's eyes lock onto mine and a strange tingling sensation overcomes me. My hands move on their own, as if they don't belong to me. I take the cup and sip. A strange lassitude washes over me within seconds, overtaking my limbs with a heavy sensation. A rose-colored hue dances through the air around me. I struggle to focus, alarmed by this sudden and odd lethargy that's taken hold of me.

I force myself to sit up straight and pretend to sip more wine to appease the dryad staring at me. Two nymphs approach Amphinome, and her gaze sharpens before they whisk her up to the moss-covered floor beneath our feet. Music plays softly in the background as they dance with her, then it becomes louder and more enticing. She's pulled in, and I watch them as they caress every inch of her body.

My face reddens from shock when I see more of them coupling. Dyname still sits eating, seemingly unaware. To be immortal and hold such innocence—is it a curse or a gift? I cannot tell.

The nymphs come to me next and pull me up. They dance around me, but Clotho's face remains clear in my mind, and while I dance, I keep my distance. Carya comes with the chalice again and bids me to sip. The strange feeling from before intensifies as I try to dance instead of drink, but I freeze in place, and she forces the liquid down my throat. I thrash back and drop the cup to the ground. My world spins and soon my eyes are in line with the chalice resting on the mossy floor beneath me.

Smiling dryads draw nearer, where skin meets skin in an innocent guise. Carya remains focused on me, and I don't know why. They pick me up and dance me further away from the center of the glade into a small circle of willow trees. I beg their leave with courteous words, and their plumb rose-colored lips pout, but they withdraw for now, leaving me lying there among the willows.

I watch the hanging branches trickle with golden light. My head continues to spin, and Carya is over me. I feel her body press against mine as she whispers sweet nothings in my ear. I hold resolve and grab her hands up and away. "Get off me," but she persists and strips naked. Fingers glide to her core, and she plays with herself, attempting to arouse me.

I do not care how beautiful she thinks she is. She is not Clotho. The wine dulls my actions further, and she straddles me, thrusting her hips into mine, and bringing my hands to her breasts. Her face gets closer and lingers near my lips. I whisper, "Stop this. I am Clotho's."

Carya's face contorts with anger. Clearly, she is not used to rejection. She digs her nails into my arms, and I howl out. She forces a kiss on my lips, and my body goes limp. The smile on her face turns feral as resistance fades away.

Her hands move to undo clasps as sugared words fill my senses. She has my pants and is pulling them down. I struggle as panic sets in, and it lends me a new strength to fling her off. My legs tremble as I try to stand. Her patience wears thin, and she snaps, lunging forward with teeth bared. She knocks me back and screeches. "I will have you."

"No, you won't."

I muster up the strength to move, my grip tightening on the trunks of the willow trees. I try to make my way out, but Carya comes up behind me and tugs at my arms. I fight to get out of her grasp, but the wine is too strong. I cannot let this demon of a woman have any inch of me. I struggle forward, moving as best I can.

I shout. “I belong to Clotho and none shall have me save for her!”

The sweet churning of the ocean fills my ears next. Amphinome’s voice overcomes the dread that was building inside as Carya inches closer. Whatever she is singing halts Carya’s madness, and she drags me away, freeing me from the dryad’s grasp. Magic veils our flight into the deepening wood. I stagger, poison clinging fast to frayed nerves.

Only Clotho’s light shines a path through dizzying shadows as we flee the dryads’ glade with traps attempting to steal our speed. My foot sinks into a hole, but Dyname quickly pulls me out. As threats pursue us both, seen and unseen, I focus on my love and I swear by Clotho’s grace alone, our purpose holds true to the course as we wend our way through the trees. Again, these sisters take on my mortal weight and guide me through this maze.

“We must get out of here, and fast,” Dyname bellows.

I try to speak in agreement, but my lips prove to be weakened by the sweet notes in that treacherous wine that bitch forced down my throat. Carya circles like a rabid beast, lust and rage twisting her beautiful face into something horrifying. Her teeth seem razor-sharp and her eyes glow red. Her naked body sprouts vines that shoot out in all directions. One wraps around my ankle and tugs me back. The twins fight back and Amphinome calls forth rippling magic to shield me while Dyname brandishes sharpened shells in each hand. Those tiny weapons cut through the vine and set me free.

Their defense buys me the time needed to gain steady footing. I force my fingers down my throat and vomit up whatever ilk remained in my stomach—hoping the spell it has on me lessens.

"You dare to break your promises, Carya? I will make Poseidon and Ares aware." Amphinome's voice carries regal authority despite the wood nymph's fury. Seeing the balance tip in our favor, I lean on my friend, who's shown her truest colors.

Though my body is less heavy and more mobile, I fight a mind still whirling. The nereid's energy seems to calm and lends me enough clarity to stumble onward. The light of the glade slowly fades into the darkness of night. We are back out in the forest where we first met Carya, and our only goal is to reach the beach on the other side.

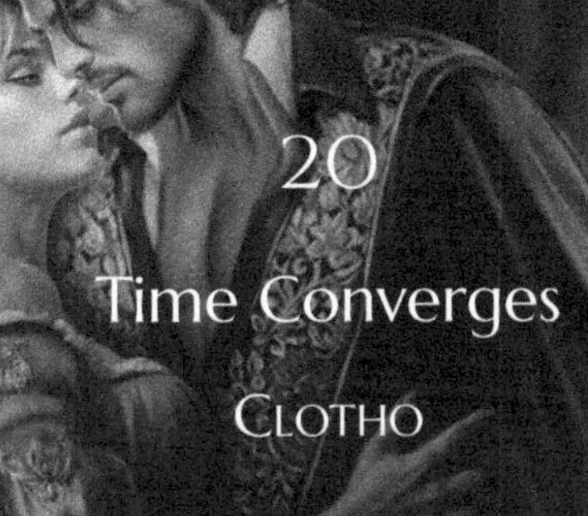

20

Time Converges

Clotho

Maximus, Cerberus, and I climb out of the ferry. Kharon holds it steady to the rocky, jagged edge of the land. He reaches for my hand and grasps it tightly. "Are you ready for this?" he asks.

"Are any of us?" I question in return. How does one prepare to face a Titan, a primordial being so old that not even time and space can truly hold him? Kharon stares knowingly into my eyes, into my soul. The worry drips off him like heavy rainfall.

"I will be fine," I tell him.

"I hope so." He doesn't doubt my abilities but knows what and who I face is greater than Zeus himself. It took Zeus and all his siblings to take Cronos down. Yet, Zeus has tasked one Moira to do the same? All because I dared to love a human. I'd repeat the night I met Marcellus over, even if I knew where this was leading. My heart belongs to Marcellus and always will. This love we share is everything. If only the immortals could see the value in loving freely.

I release my friend's hand and go forward. Kharon shouts my name. "Clotho!"

"Yes, old friend?"

"You will tame Cronos. I know it."

I nod my head as the ferry leaves us on unknown shores. My only companions now are two very determined dogs. I giggle. Is this a small gift from Hecate herself? I am honored if it is so. I never thought so many immortals would be on my side. But I must ask myself how they all know? I bet Zeus hopes to make a mockery out of me and has spread what I have done far and wide.

Iaso said they were none the wiser. So, who followed her and spied? I want to know, but I doubt I'll ever find out. Maximus strides ahead, then returns to my side. Cerberus follows, and I pet them both. I am in the best company. Loyalty is not a question with these two.

The landscape ahead begins to shift and change. The rocky beach gives way to tall grasses and budding flowers. There is something different about the place we've entered. The sand from the beach swirls through the air.

At first, the sand is like the dusting of fireflies dancing in the night sky, but then it takes thicker forms, vaguely humanoid. They drift and transform before dissipating, the granules falling to the ground. Patches of thick fog appear in clusters, swelling rapidly, obscuring the path we take only to vanish as suddenly as they came.

Monolithic stone pillars chiseled from obsidian appear off in the distance. The sky above darkens and flashes auroras of sickly greens and purples, making the grass and flowers glow an eerie bioluminescent hue. Geometric structures emerge from the earth, and clusters of half-buried crystals are revealed. They hum and vibrate on some unknown frequency I cannot hear, but my companions shake their heads from the pitch they are hearing. I try to calm them as the landscape morphs again.

The ground we walk on rises and turns us round and round. Sense of time and direction are distorted. I survey our environment, noticing unfamiliar constellations scattered across the heavens. Perceptions of the past and future intermingle with the foliage surrounding us.

I see Marcellus in his mask, asking me to dance. Then I am in the cave with Pythia as she tells me how I'll be my own undoing. There are other scenes I don't recognize with people and faces I do not know. I can tell we are getting closer to where Cronos resides.

Cerberus steps in front of me and growls. The land protrudes spiky, clear shards. This mayhem would leave me lost and wounded without these two.

Maximus nudges my hand, and I rest my palm on the top of his head. He senses my unease. His stable energy comforts me as we trudge toward chaos itself.

So far, there is not another soul save for the apparitions that appear and disappear around us. Maximus and Cerberus stick close to me and guide me through the changes that keep happening. Night becomes day, then night once more, blinding light followed by pitch black—I cannot see my hand in front of me. I feel them on either side now, leading me safely to the next convergence.

The darkness seems unending. Much like the cave of oracles, there is a dense energy growing stronger in the air. A dim light sticks out ahead, and I head toward it. There is enough light to see the dogs on either side of me. The ground beneath our feet shifts less, but mounds of dirt rise in front of us. At first, they appear to be nothing more than what they seem, but pointy teeth and gnarled faces poke out and spring forth with tiny blades held in boxy waxen hands.

Whatever these creatures are, their skin is stretched translucent over twisted ropey muscles coiled beneath their sallow forms. Beady eyes glitter with dim intelligence and malice. Their sickly blueish hued skin has a faint glow to it. Blade-like claws extend from their gangly fingertips.

They erupt one after another from the earth, a nightmarish chorus of hisses and clicks emanating from their malformed throats. Bones rattle against each other as their stiff limbs propel them in our direction. Their eyes lock on us with a single-mindedness. We are now their prey.

Maximus howls, and Cerberus braces himself against the ground. Low growls rumble from both their chests, and fur bristles along their spines as their lips peel back to reveal gleaming white canines. They dart ahead to intercept our attackers, meeting twisted ferocity with focused defense. Teeth and claws clash in flashes. One strike after another, snapping jaws clamp down tight on enemies' legs. Limbs fly and blood sprays. Shock envelopes me. I have witnessed no battle in depth, not up close like this.

Maximus snatches one creature by the torso and tosses it before rounding back where I am frozen, unable to move. He barks, the sound commanding and full of force. I have no weapon, so I ready my fists, but my companions battle to shield me while I prep for what comes next.

I glance down and smile. Taking hold of a knotted limb pried loose in the fray, wielding it as a makeshift club against clutching talons and snapping mouths. A wet crunch rewards a well-placed blow, and my stomach pulses with disgust.

Maximus tears one apart in a flurry of slashing teeth and paws, flinging pieces that twitch and reform on the soil. Cerberus adopts a defensive stance before me, his three maws foaming as he lets loose a draconic roar that makes the creatures hesitate before they lunge forward. But hunger and instinct override fear, compelling the creatures ever closer in a scrabbling, shambling press. Dark magic animates limbs ripped from torsos, granting new vessels for their malevolent wills. We are outnumbered, and the dogs grow weary under the relentless assault.

All seems lost, but a beacon pulses within my soul. The Moirai gifts stir, answering an unspoken call for help, and I know my sisters are with me. Golden light bursts from my being in searing cords that encircle the horde. The creatures' forms convulse, warping unnaturally before dissolving into the dirt whence they came.

Peace settles on the plain, and my companions lean against my legs, tongues lolling as the magic's cost takes hold. I falter in my steps, and Cerberus takes me softly in his jaws and rests me on a flattened stone. I know we cannot stay here much longer. Maximus pushes me onto Cerberus's back.

Tears roll down my cheeks. I am so lucky to have these two right now. We hurry onward in this shrouded realm of Cronos's making, toward our fated confrontation. I only hope we can outmaneuver what happens next.

21

Staying Grounded

Clotho

The once expansive plains become a hooded forest with tangled vines suffocating the trees and blocking out the sunlight. The ground is littered with tiny pebbles that hover around, barely touching the soil beneath them. Wildflowers sprout from cracks in the earth, quickly blossoming, wilting, and dying before the cycle starts again. Gravity behaves strangely, lurching at odd angles. Only the dogs keep me grounded and oriented. I have no idea how I'm supposed to defeat Cronos.

Even now, I can feel his gaze observing us from beyond perception, an eldritch presence scrutinizing our every step toward the confrontation that awaits us at journey's end. An icy chill reverberates up my spine, spreading throughout my limbs. The fine hairs on my neck and arms rise in protest. The unpleasant sensation persists. Wave after wave of freezing shudders rack my frame.

Something deep within me has been breached, unleashing this torrent of frozen dread into my very bones. I cannot shake the feeling. As we traverse the shifting landscapes, the dogs notice my worsening condition. They press closer, sharing warmth and steadying my trembling form. Though the encroaching cold seeps deep, their spirits bolster my resolve.

Up ahead, the forest thins out and unveils a clearing filled with an eerie silence. Stone columns circle a sheer-walled chamber from which yawns an opening into fathomless shadow. A primal force vibrates the very air, its essence intensifying my tremors.

We stand before the mouth of Cronos's sanctuary. Within that inky abyss, his chaos reigns supreme. I can sense his reality-bending will press upon me even as I sense his restraint. Some great trial awaits, and I hope I have the fortitude to face what the Titan throws at us next.

Maximus and Cerberus sense my uncertainty. Their calming energy encourages me to move forward, and together, we enter the clearing. Their furry bodies provide me warmth and shield me from surrendering to the bitter cold as we penetrate the depths of Cronos's new domain.

Clutching their comforting forms, I call forth my innate powers, determined to confront the manifestations the Titan will throw our way. A dark mist rises from the ground, and we are bathed in its darkness within seconds. I summon the grace of my sister Fates as we plunge farther into the unknown.

With each step closer to Cronos, the unnatural quiet intensifies. The gloom of the mist lifts just enough to make out the path in front of us. The utter silence enveloping us is deafening. Not even the echo of our footsteps disturbs this deadened void. An eerie stillness unlike any realm I've been in blankets the air, smothering all sensation besides the cold still passing through my veins.

The uncanny calm magnifies my dread. No worldly phenomenon compares to the fear seeping into my soul's core. Through the murk, I glimpse a glowing rim surrounding a vast chamber ahead. Within that glacial aura, an entity of nightmarish proportions awaits our arrival.

My heart is pounding and my breath hitches in my throat. As we push through to the entrance, a fierce gust of wind rushes towards us and whips by, ripping at my skin—like the thorns of wild rose bushes, pricking the flesh. I look down at my arms. I flinch as it tears open my skin, leaving tiny cuts that blossom with beads of blood. Even the air is dangerous in this place. Cronos's power intensifies the closer we get.

I have no idea how I will overcome him. But there is no turning back now.

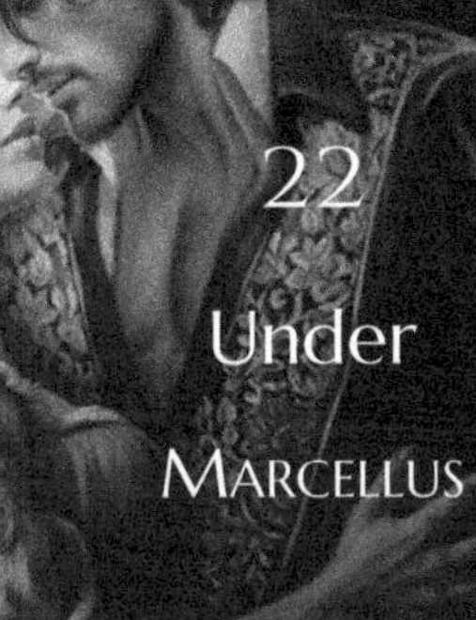

22

Under

Marcellus

As we continue journeying through the dense woods, shadows deepen around us with every step we take. Underneath the tightly woven canopy, the pale moon only offers faint glimpses of its light. Amphinome curses under her breath. "Damn Carya and her nymphs all the way to the Underworld. May Hades take her for this betrayal."

Dyname agrees, as do I, but deep down, I knew something wasn't right. I know not all immortals will be as helpful as these two, and not every being we meet will be on our side. Fate seems to be on my side, yet I am in this situation because I dared to love the very embodiment of it.

I long to feel Clotho's lips on mine, to see the way she lights up with a smile when I am near. Those thoughts drive me forward. If anything, I must succeed and make it back to her in one piece.

To think, moments ago, that dryad tried to sink her claws in and turn me into something I am not. Some part of me feels foolish for thinking I could find sanctuary with them—if even for a little bit. Even now, my body craves rest. Rest I am sure I will not get.

Carya's loyalty lies with Zeus, and the test of our love began far before Iaso came to warn us—that much is evident. My head spins while I try to gain my footing once again. Whatever they put in that wine is pure poison. I hope to never encounter another dryad in my lifetime. Even then, it will be too soon.

The twins help me along until the wine clears more from my body. Our pace quickens as I regain full functionality once more.

"We need to get you to the closest entryway to the Underworld," Amphinome whispers.

"To the waters then," Dyname replies.

"What do you mean, the water? Is this the reason for the gift earlier?" I ask, curious to know more details.

They speak in unison. "Yes. We need to hurry. Minos and his beast still trail us, alongside Carya."

I nod in response when I hear the distant sounds of a large animal, which I assume is none other than the Chimera. We swiftly take off, heading north. Each step I take, I take with care and with as much speed as possible without creating unnecessary noise. The twins do the same. I barely breathe as we continue toward our destination.

The closer we get to the ocean, the safer we will be. My nerves are frayed, but I focus on the goal I wish to obtain. I wonder what I will encounter once I reach Hades' domain. Will luck be on my side, and I'll meet Kharon right away? Or will more grueling tests present themselves to me? Will the twins see me off and leave me to find my way alone? I need to ask, but now is not the time. I hear Minos and his demon getting closer. My blood boils. While I do not want to tangle with either, I'd gladly stick my dagger right through his neck next time.

I hope his kind is unwelcome deep in the sea, that we can embark into the depths without him following, but I know better. He will chase me until Zeus commands him otherwise. I'd stab the god-king in his neck, too, if I had the chance. I take men at their actions, not just their words.

And Zeus is not a man of his word. He'll spit out one thing and do the opposite. He thinks all mortals are foolish, but there are those of us watching the gods on the mounts with intense scrutiny.

I am sure the same can be said of the gods themselves. I never thought Poseidon would help me. My thoughts turn to him, and I mumble a small thank you. In Roma, we are taught to give thanks right away when we are given something from the Olympians. I only hope my hushed words meet his ears.

Once I resolve everything, I will take the time to pay my respects, showing my gratitude and appreciation. I cling to optimism in these fleeting seconds, hoping for the best. I glide nimbly through the thinning wood. The beach comes into view peeking out between the tree line. But the hairs on the nape of my neck stand erect, and an enormous snake's head slithers across my arm and upper chest. An icy chill reverberates up the length of my spine.

Our enemies have found us. Fuck the quiet of our steps. Dyname screams at the top of her lungs and slaps the Chimera's tail into the dirt. The head hisses and spits in protest. I whirl around, looking back to see where Minos is. His furious eyes meet mine, and I make sure not to react.

There is no way we can try to fight them. I tug at Dyname's arm as her sister darts ahead of us. "Let's go!"

We sprint to the opening of the trees, greeted by the sandy beach beneath our feet. I feel myself sink in and try my best to keep pace. The sisters are more graceful and glide with ease to the water's edge. We are almost there. I can taste freedom from Minos's grasp.

Minos roars from the tree line. "I'll skin you alive for what you did to me!"

It would be foolish to turn around and pay him any heed. Under the veil of moonlight, I trudge forward along the shore; the water lapping up to my feet. As I go further out into the water, the sky lightens. All the stars brighten up like noonday's sun. Confused by this sudden change, I come to a halt and realize that day has fully replaced night. What kind of magic is at play here that the very world shifts around me? Were the rumors true then? Is it the Titan, Cronos, entering our world, as Iaso told Clotho and me?

I sense the Chimera close to me, and without thinking, I hurriedly make a dive into the shallows and start swimming away. Amphinome tells me to dive deeper. The beast paddles after me with such speed. I am not sure when this gift of hers will kick in.

She must sense my unease. "You need to fully submerge yourself until you feel yourself running out of air, then your body will switch over."

The information is not lost on me as I dive deeper and swim further down. I see the Chimera trying to follow me, but it struggles and swims back up. Light from above shifts once more, and it is night again, making it harder to see the enemy. My arms and legs burn from pushing past the currents and further into the sea.

I spot Minos swimming to me now, but I keep going. No obstacles or challenges will deter me from reaching the Underworld. My focus is unwavering as I persist toward my goal: the sweet embrace of Clotho in my arms.

The twins swirl around me as we advance farther into Poseidon's domain. Minos's feeble attempts to grab me fail time and again. His muddled growls steal the air from him, and I watch him shoot up to the surface.

Free from his pursuit, I plunge down and await the transformation. My lungs are already burning. A pins and needles sensation creeps through my limbs, and a heaviness overcomes my entire body. Panic sets in. My heart is racing, ears throbbing from the pressure of the ocean upon me.

My mouth gasps open and water pours in. My vision tunnels, but I see Dyname and Amphinome swimming to aid me.

Like the moment we met, they are on either side guiding me down, down, deep. Muffled words fill my ears at first, but then they are clear as day. "Breathe the water in again. Embrace the gift fully."

I take in salt water; it's burning my nostrils. I push it in and out. My heavy limbs start to feel light and free. The tingling remains for a moment, but then a sharp, lacerating pain shoots through the sides of my neck, and instinctively, I reach up. Instead of smooth skin, there are gills like a fish.

My fingers ache as I watch flesh grow between them. The twins are smiling like mad at me as I stare down in disbelief. My transformation is complete. The weight I felt from the water lifts, and I swim around freely.

Above us, Minos and the Chimera struggle to reach us—always going back up for air. Released from their torment for the time being, I relish the newfound freedom and reprieve from their attack. Amphinome beckons me to follow her as she swirls down further into Poseidon's domain.

There are amazing sights to see. Large, tree-like seaweed rocks back and forth like there is a breeze. Octopi and fish of all colors swim by. I even spot a shark hunting near a large reef.

The beauty below the surface completely entrances me. Few mortals have the pleasure of seeing this world up-close. Even amid challenging circumstances, I consider myself lucky to gaze upon what most people only dream of.

The deeper we go, the more the scenery changes and gloom surrounds us. I follow closely behind the twins, consciously aware I am encroaching on areas unknown to a mortal like me, where sleeping giants wait for their prey.

I've heard many tales of the monsters at sea. The ones in the deepest crevices of the ocean where we are now swimming. It is only a matter of time before we encounter such a creature.

Somehow, my thoughts instantly become reality. A swarm of writhing tentacles erupts from a deep chasm somewhere down below. There is just enough light for me to make out the thickness of each appendage, like the massive trees in the Hercynian Forest.

The twins dart out of the way, and I follow their movement. We swoop down and loop around four of the limbs before zooming up into a narrow canyon.

Dyname speaks. "Don't worry about Scylla. She's harmless ... on a good day."

My mouth gapes open: *Scylla,* the famed monster of the eight seas! With a rush of adrenaline, my heart pounds in my chest, filling me with a potent combination of terror and exhilaration. My gaze shoots back to see a giant eye tracking our every move, and fear washes over me like a wave of icy water, crashing against my skin and leaving me shivering and breathless in its wake. Yet when I stare deeper into the eye of Scylla, a strange calm overcomes me.

Legends only scratch at the surface of the beast's true nature. She gazes at me with a serene, all-knowing eye. Her wisdom and intellect radiate from her very being. I cannot explain how I am able to sense these things, but it is as if she's passing a message along to me.

As her large eye blinks, a comforting voice floods my thoughts with soothing words. *Strength be with you.*

I am left speechless by the message reserved for me from such an ancient being.

There are those who have so much faith in the love Clotho and I share. This faith keeps me going. Some people would judge a man in his forties pursuing a love often reserved for the youth. But their opinions hold no weight over my heart.

Though there were many that told me my love had come and gone, I care not.

Some would also think I am too old to face the gods as I do now. I pity their limited perspective. I may not be as mighty as Hercules or as heroic as Perseus, but my determination knows no bounds when it comes to pursuing whom I love.

For age is merely a number, a construct of society rooted in mortality. But the soul is infinite, knowing no bounds of time or physical limitations. And my connection with Clotho transcends the mundane constraints placed on us by the world's expectations.

I watch Scylla before she disappears below the canyon's plunging depths. We glide through the pass without further obstruction.

I never knew there could be such silence beneath the ocean. Our strokes make brief sounds in this confined gorge. Along the ledges, there is no sign of plant life, only a barren landscape of sand and rocks. Their grayish hues turn to pitch black the farther we travel inward.

The twins turn to me. "We are almost there."

A strange thumping, much like a slowed heartbeat, starts out low, barely audible to my ears. The closer we come to the Underworld, the louder the rhythmic pulse gets. There is nothing else, just the beat reverberating through every limb.

The pulsing grows louder, its dreadful rhythm burrowing deeper into my bones with every stroke. Where previously curiosity swirled, now only icy tendrils of fear claw their way through my veins.

The path continues to narrow, plunging us into utter blackness. No light penetrates the abyss in which we are cocooned. The twins' luminescence is the only beacon of reassurance, but even then, their glow begins to dim with each downward flick of their tails. I fear their light will fade, leaving us encased in this suffocating night that threatens to smother the bravery within me.

That relentless pounding now fills my skull to bursting, a maddening march that surely leads us straight to some nameless doom. A sliver of thought pierces my brain. Why did I agree to delve into realms forbidden to mortal flesh?

Some part of me wishes to flee, to scream, yet the terror that builds deep inside holds me mute and motionless. Dyname tugs at my wrist, ushering me forward. But I am stuck in a trance—the endless cavern exudes an aura of ancient malice, seeping deeper into my core with each beat. My veins continue to run painfully cold, and I force my heart to beat slowly. I fear that if it beats any faster it will join the hellish cadence, and escape from this torment will never come. I'll be trapped in the ocean's oblivion for eternity.

The cavern yawns wide before us, and a sickly light seeps from an unseen source, illuminating a nightmarish vision. Suspended in the rock is an obscene growth, a pulsing membrane of veined flesh protruding outward. My body locks in revulsion. This throbbing mass is the source of that maddening beat.

Its surface ripples and swells, straining against some invisible pressure. I steel myself and swim toward this ghastly abomination. The veins flush from purple to black in a mere second, and I stop once more.

Amphinome lays a comforting hand on my shoulder. "The entrance awaits. You've been brave. Come, it is time to pass from this world into the Nether."

For a moment, I consider begging them to leave, to let us flee this damnable place, but Clotho awaits. I cannot give in to the terror that threatens to choke the very life from me. I picture her face and fuel my determination once more, despite the horror creeping through my form.

"You must swim through the Visceral Veil to reach the Underworld." Amphinome motions me forward. I say nothing. She senses my hesitation. "Do not stop now. This is meant to deter you from the way forward."

"Will you and Dyname be coming with me?" I ask.

"Sadly, no. This is where we part ways, my friend, but trust that Kharon will guide you going forward. Find the Ferryman immediately." They both push me toward the fleshy gate, and I cringe. My fingers outstretched, I touch the edges and feel my stomach curdling.

"Go! Before it is too late!" Dyname screams. I am confused by their urgency, but then I see shadowy beasts crawling down the canyon walls.

"What about you two? I can't leave you to face these creatures without me!"

"Don't worry about us!" They push my body with such force I feel the squirming of the flesh pod on my right side.

"Thank you both," I say before I take a deep breath and plunge the rest of my body through, leaving my friends to tangle with creatures unknown.

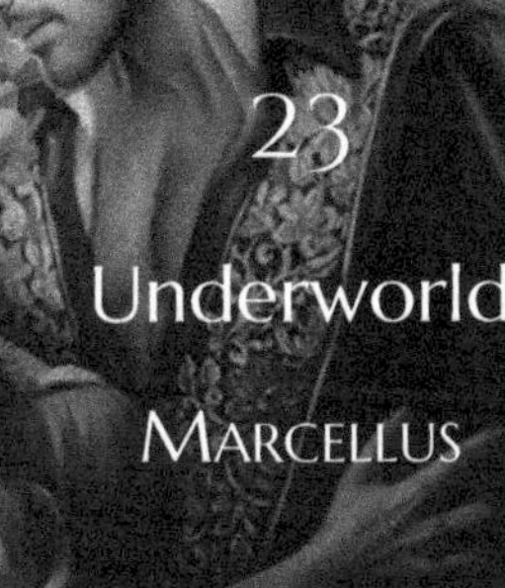

23
Underworld
Marcellus

I reach the other side, and it is no longer a vast ocean, but a cave illuminated by shimmering crystals and a river with a faint glow. The shock of the switch causes me to lose my breath. The gills on my neck tighten, and the webbed skin between my extremities shrink. I choke out a muffled howl, spitting up salt water. I fall to my knees and swear I must be dying. The webbed skin has disappeared completely, and the gills seal up on my neck.

I gasp for air and crumple to the ground in a heap of pain. Nothing prepared me for the transition from water back to land. If anything, this transformation was worse than the first. The water burned but quickly became gentle. The air pricks my lungs like a thousand knives.

It takes me several minutes to adjust to the crippling dryness of the Underworld. I chuckle at the idea of this place being arid when, in reality, there is a dank scent permeating the landscape about me. As my eyes adjust to the eerie glow, I gaze upon a realm like nothing I've seen before. Jagged stalactites cradle sulfurous fires, casting malevolent shadows across the cavern walls. Beyond the river lies a barren, ashen field, as sun starved as the deepest depths of the sea I left.

Shambling, skeletal-like creatures seven feet tall drift through the gloom, obscured by grayish wisps of cloth that shroud their faces. Phantasms with curling smoky tails float up from the riverbed, and cloaked figures wander listlessly along the riverbank. Lost souls scarred beyond recognition as the people they once were.

An aura of unspeakable suffering exudes from these twisted beings, their formless moans raising the hairs on the nape of my neck.

Not even Scylla's presence had me shivering with this much dread.

A movement in the waters catches my eye. Pale green forms tangle together, grasping desperately to each other as the current bears them onward into an unending abyss. Their numbers swell, and the water line rises. An endless parade of the damned cry out with unseen torment. I recoil from the water's edge, those spectral wails, like sharp talons, scraping down my spine. I walk along the river, ever mindful of the dreadful souls clamoring not too far from me. I look for something to guide me to where I need to go, but I have no idea if the Underworld is like Aetheria. Are there signs that lead me to my destination, or will I be stuck wandering until my death?

I decide to take the path down the most lit cavern, where the river's mouth widens. The gloom dissipates, while the miserable souls in the water persist. It's as if they follow me, hoping I can save them from their agony. I force myself to ignore their pleas for help and travel further down, praying I spot the Ferryman soon.

Again, the river expands, and I spot the ferry's post across a vast pool. Several other streams lead into it, and I wonder if these other paths are like the one I am on. How do I reach the other side without plunging into that festering flood of ichor and despair? As if sensing my dilemma, the murk roils. Skeletal hands emerge, clawing towards me. Soulless eyes glare up from pallid faces, pleading voices curdling my marrow.

I turn to run, but the atrophied bodies lay siege to me. Screeching erupts from the roiling river. The fleshless limbs flail as tattered souls climb up the bank, a hellish light glinting off their bones.

With a cry, the first wraith latches its bony fingers around my ankle. I kick furiously at its feeble grip, but there is something spiritual hanging on. Another being emerges and seizes my arm with a forceful grip. Panic rises in my throat. I grapple with their jointless holds, but more gaunt hands tear at my clothes. Their wretched moans merge into an unsettling dirge. Their cursed souls pull incessantly at my flesh.

The dark water churns before my eyes as the corpses worm their way ever higher. There must be hundreds, if not thousands. Bony claws lash out, scraping my skin. Blood trickles along my forearm, and for a split second, I wish the throng of decrepit beings were none other than Minos. At least I know his weakness, but how do I stop these denizens of the Nether from holding me down?

I use all the strength left in me to pull myself away, but the forces these damned souls carry keep me bound to them. I pick up a large stone and smash it into several skulls. Shattered pieces fly everywhere, and for a single moment, I think I am free—but the pieces wiggle, twist, and coil like frenzied serpents. Shards of bone zip through the murk with a supernatural speed, each fragment finding its way back to its host.

Jagged edges click into place, knitting back together in a gristly puzzle. Some sort of flesh bubbles forth, filling in the fractural fissures with a leathery membrane.

The cracked skulls are now whole as they once were.

I freeze in terror, realizing that there is no escape from my newest enemy. More rotting and skeletal hands take hold of me, dragging me closer to the river's edge. I fight back the best I can. "Clotho, I cannot let these beings have me now when I am so close!" I bellow. The writhing hoard engulfs me, its relentless force slamming my body against the unforgiving rocks. The agony of my skin being torn open is unbearable, and the scent of blood hangs thick in the air.

"Fresh blood," a remnant gurgles close to my ear. I shudder. The smell of decay wafts past my nostrils, and bile builds in the back of my throat. I lurch from the stench, still battling every single hand that has me in its grasp.

I cannot give in. The water soaks me up to my knees. I am losing. They tug once more, and I am immersed in their slimy existence. But water fills my mouth, and the nereid's gift comes forth. My weakened limbs find new vigor, and I spring forward, swimming to reach the other side where the ferry awaits me.

The lost souls meld together into a distorted blob and roll toward me, thrashing and churning as they come after me. I push myself harder as gangling hands rip at my limbs. I advance, but they are not far behind. The urgency to reach the other side intensifies. I try diving deeper into the water to escape the warped mass of tattered entities. They are relentless in their pursuit of my soul, and the fear within me builds as much as the pressure to reach my destination does.

Some of the wretched phantoms break off from the group and spiral downward in my direction. I change my course and shoot back up to the water's surface. All the while, they pile atop each other, a churning avalanche of spectral flesh raging toward me.

They writhe about like snakes, grasping desperately to claim my essence. A vortex of pale limbs and shriveled faces will forever haunt me if I make it out alive.

Every muscle in my body screams, but I press on. I haven't come this far to lose my soul to the howling maelstrom fed by the unending tide of damned spirits now.

No, I must make it to the other side.

Bony fingers claw at my sides again as the soul mound surges round me. Panic sets in, and I scream out her name. *Clotho!* If this is to be my end, let her name be the last thing on my lips. My bottom half collides with the pallid sea of screaming faces. I fight back at my adversaries, lungs burning for the air denied me.

A surge of strength emerges from desperation. With a gasp, I manage to pull my head above their crushing mass. I kick my legs to keep myself afloat. I thrash my arms around and push myself up. A small sliver of resolve enters me, but a force below drags me back down.

Blackness crawls into my vision, but among the murk of eternal death I see a gleam—a lantern's hope where none should be.

Something grabs my shoulders in an iron grip, wrenching me free from the ghouls' raking nails. Breaking me free from the hellish crusade. I fight to breathe, coughing up bile and spitting up the sludge that surrounded me. By some cosmic grace, I am alive. I look up to see who saved me, and staring down at me is the Ferryman of the River Styx.

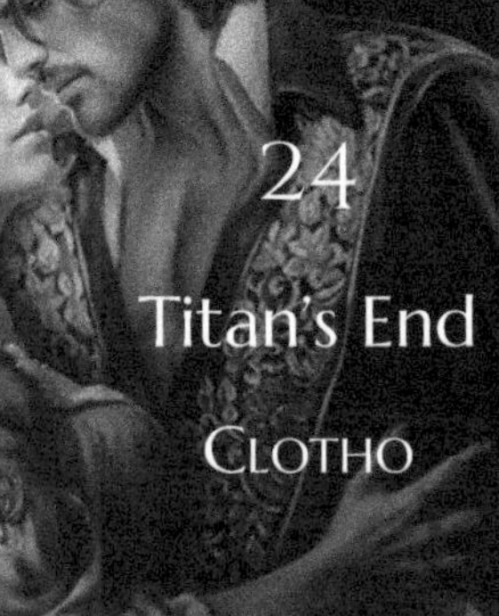

24

Titan's End

Clotho

The strange aura in front of us pulsates with an otherworldly energy, solid yet ethereal. Its peculiar glow casts a violet shadow on the walls. The entrance is too small for Cerberus to enter. His massive form looms behind me as he lets out a whimper. I reach out and place my hand on one of his heads, feeling the softness of his ebony fur beneath my fingertips. I stroke his three heads affectionately. "Thank you for your unwavering assistance on this dangerous journey. I couldn't have done this without you and Maximus by my side. Go to Kharon now. Maybe you can help Marcellus next when he arrives?"

I glance over at Maximus. His ears perk up at the mention of his master's name. His eyes shift from me to Cerberus.

Cerberus hesitates and lets out a small whine. Maximus edges closer to him and nudges him, almost like he is saying, it is okay.

"I promise we will be fine, but I am worried about Marcellus. Please guide him to us?"

Cerberus seems to accept my suggestion while I rub his ears. I send one last message into Cerberus' mind: *Marcellus will be missing his Max, I am sure. But he will be excited to know that you were with us, and he is even better at giving pets than I am!*

I glance over at Maximus. "You can go, too. If you'd like." I tell him, but he gently nips my wrists and sits in front of me, staring up with eyes so full of intent I now know why he will not leave my side.

"Marcellus commanded you to stay with me no matter what, didn't he?" I ask.

He barks. The sound is short and punchy, as if he is saying yes. But I worry about him coming with me. He must not be harmed.

"I will not stop you, but your safety matters to me," I tell him, scratching behind his ears.

Maximus leans into the scratches, relishing the attention, his tail wagging happily. He groans with contentment before I wrap my arms around him. "Thank you," I whisper.

I know this loyal canine's resolve. He will stay by my side, no matter what.

"Ready?" I ask.

Maximus barks short and quick. A firm yes if I ever heard one.

I waver for a moment, knowing the challenge will not be easy. I cannot let a shred of uncertainty enter my being. Not if I want to succeed. Maximus goes up to Cerberus, and they nudge each other before we depart. My heart is heavy as we watch the beast of Hades head back the way we came.

Surety is the only way. I remind myself of my inherent gifts—that I am not alone, my sisters' energies are also with me. Some will always see the Fates below the Olympians. Yet they all fail to realize who controls their threads. Even the mighty Titan Cronos cannot tangle with a Moira without consequences. I am unsure of what those would be, but I've sent out messages to my sisters and brother. Now I must face my trial to make the world right. I steady my nerves and call on Fates past, present, and future to aid me in what happens next. Then I take a step into the cavern where the Father of Time has chosen to reside.

The pathway is long and narrow. Pearlescent walls threaten to crush me before I reach the other end. A gravelly voice cracks in the distance. "Come in.".

It vibrates through the passage we are in and ripples through every inch of my body and soul. Maximus growls, taking a protective stance directly in front of me. The final opening is several steps ahead. My feet slow. I have no real plan besides convincing the Titan that I'm on his side. But eons in a prison of his son's own making have twisted the once amiable soul.

Prophecy also took away the love Cronos had for his children. Distorting everything he once held dear, leading him to his own doom. Truth be told, I am in similar shoes and must face what I have done. I am here because of my choices. I am not sure of my chances, but I hold on to Kharon's words of hope. He thinks I have a chance, so I muster the courage to believe the same. I also cannot fathom shattering my true love's heart if I'm defeated.

I'm doing this for him, for us, and for the future yet to come.

I know my actions have consequences. A single thread led me here to this moment.

A crime I'd gladly commit again. I remember being so young and naïve in Pythia's cave. So afraid of the vision shown to me, I didn't truly live. Maybe more good can come from my supposed mistake. But I am not even sure it is one. The only fault I see now is not letting myself love to begin with. Centuries of holding back, of letting fear keep its grip on me.

But if I hadn't steeled myself against humans for so long, would I have met Marcellus?

Perhaps things happen for a reason. I take a few more steps forward.

It's time.

I will not prolong the inevitable any longer.

I step through the final opening, Maximus close at my side. A behemoth of a man looms before us—Cronos, his immense form taking up a sizable portion of the cavernous space surrounding us. He sits upon a throne crafted from gnarled roots and twisted branches, a testament to the ancient power he possesses. The bark cracks, revealing what appears to be lava inside each crevice. If this is true, the heat permeating from its depths does not bother him.

My eyes lock on to one side of his face, which is constantly shifting in form. It is hard to make out the changes. He is many things, young then old. The other side remains unchanging. Silver hair curls about his entire face, and a lengthy beard travels down to the middle of his chest.

The only thing covering his body is an elaborate ivory skirt that goes down to his knees. Gold and silver ink tattoo his bare chest. The design on his skin is a harvest scythe wrapping around a clock, with shafts of wheat weaving around both. The hand on the clock is moving, and lightning shoots out from the design, illuminating the pale skin across his entire torso.

My eyes travel up to his fiery gaze. "Mighty Cronos, I come before you seeking balance in this mortal realm. I am Clotho of the Moirai, a spinner of the threads of Fate."

A rumbling chuckle shakes the walls. "So, the rumor holds true. Zeus sent a goddess of destiny to deal with me this day." His eyes flare a searing gold. "And what business could one such as you have with one such as I, little sister?"

"I seek only cooperation, not conflict. Great changes have unfolded, and balance must be restored." I stand tall, showing my conviction.

Cronos leans forward, a jagged grin splitting his ashen features. "Only a fool trusts that Zeus will keep his word. What did he promise you if you succeed in taming me and returning me to Tartarus?"

I meet his burning gaze steadily. "I assume he will let me reunite with my one true love, my soul's other half, if I convince you to return."

"Ah, the human you are so enthralled with. I have seen that you have defied the rule of gods and mortals coupling. A forbidden love. Hmm." He pauses. "Few have dared to approach me with such mettle. Perhaps you can offer more than empty promises given to this Titan of old?" His eyebrow arches in challenge.

I stand unwavering, eyes locked with his own. "I have something others didn't."

Amusement touches his booming tone. "And pray tell, what is it you have that sets you apart from others, Clotho?"

"While there are gods and goddesses above me in station, I still have dominion over all threads—even theirs," I state calmly yet firmly.

A brief flicker of surprise crosses Cronos's smoldering stare. "At last, someone offers me more than words. They offer me power equal to my own, and a vast one. But how does this Moira plan to use such bait?"

"I've been told of what you want, and when the time is right and Zeus goes against his word, and he will, I will force him to do as he promises."

Cronos's lips curl into a half-smile as I approach him. "How?" he asks, stroking his large fingers through his silver beard. "There is no thread of a god on your person. Why should I trust you so blindly? Surely, little sister, deep down, you know you cannot beat Zeus. I do not think he will say yes to handing over Tartarus as my boon."

"I do not wish it to come to that. But if I must fight for myself and Marcellus, I'll do it. I will prove that our love is not lust. It is real, it is forever. It is true."

He throws back his mane of hair and roars with laughter. "You truly believe in such a thing? With a mortal?"

"I don't believe. I know."

"Such confidence, but can your faith withstand seeing your lover's true nature?" Beside him, a mirror surfaces from the shadows. I peer within and hold back a gasp.

The mirror ripples. I see Marcellus lying on his back and a woman straddling him. She is naked and holds his hands to her breasts.

My heart wrenches for a second, but I know the dryads and nymphs. That was Carya. *The worst of their bunch.* She spikes her victims' wine and takes many without their consent.

And I do not believe Marcellus gave in. I can't believe it, and I won't. "You show me but a tiny sliver in time. Where is the rest? A false vision, old god. A deceitful trick. I know my lover's heart," I say evenly, though my own twists from the glimpse given to me.

Cronos leans forward, eyes gleaming. "Are you sure? After all, mortals are fickle things."

I meet his gaze without hesitation. "Yes. Marcellus has proven his devotion time and again. He will fight for our love, against all odds. My faith in him remains unshaken."

The Titan chuckles darkly. "We shall see if your promise holds out. You make bold declarations, little Fate. Now it's time to prove yourself."

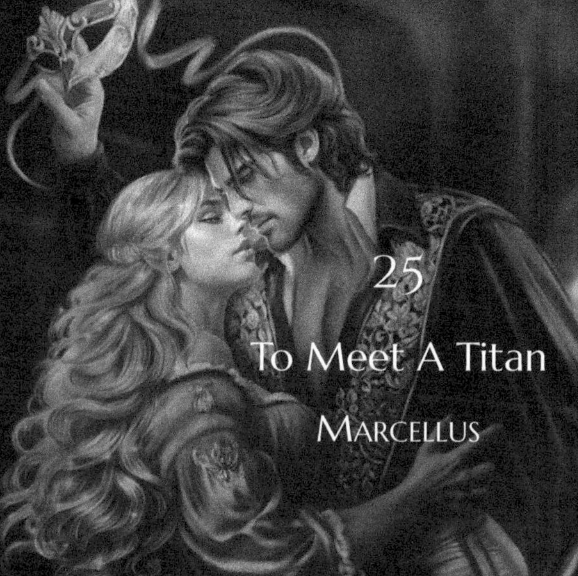

25

To Meet A Titan

Marcellus

Radiating pain rouses me from unconsciousness. I groan, squinting against the blinding light filtering down overhead. *Where am I?* The swaying motion and lapping waves trigger memories—Kharon's boat. I thought for sure the denizens of the deep swallowed me whole, but no, he pulled me out of their suffocating hell.

I pull myself up using the sides of the ferry as a rasping chuckle breaks my swirling thoughts. "Awake at last." Kharon's golden eyes meet mine.

"Clotho, I need to get to her. Where is she? I must–" My urgent question is cut off by a spidery hand close to my face.

"She faces Cronos to save you both."

I try to stand up too fast, head spinning. No, she cannot face him alone! I tumble backwards, but Kharon's gnarled grip steadies me. "Rest. You do not have your strength back."

"But–"

He puts his hand up. "Rest while we travel to his realm. Then hurry, as her thread depends on you."

I sit back down and rest my head against a large woven sack while Kharon explains Clotho's mission. She will offer Cronos something he cannot resist. It seems too good to be true, but I must trust that what she has is enough. In the meantime, it seems like Clotho and I must continue to prove our love. Every move I've made has felt like one test after another. All I know is I can't wait to stand by her side once more.

I regain enough balance to prop myself up next to Kharon. He fixes me with a peculiar stare, his unusual eyes gleaming with an unreadable expression. There is a calculating glint amid the usual cold disinterest, as if a question has surfaced that defies his understanding of the boundaries between life and death.

Sensing his scrutiny, I meet his gaze steadily. "What is it? You seem perplexed by something."

Kharon blinks slowly, as if emerging from deep contemplation. "How is it a mortal bested the wraiths of Erebus, when so many souls far older have fallen to their touch?" he rasps quietly. "How did you survive as long as you did?"

"I don't know."

A thin frown crosses his features, a tightening of ancient wrinkles spreads through his forehead. I hold no answer to sate his curious mind. But he seems satisfied with my answer, and only nods, yet I see his mind churning. I acknowledge him, then hobble over to take a seat closer to the front of the boat. I wish I had more answers, but all I know is the necessity of haste for Clotho's sake. Kharon ushers the ferry forward.

"It won't be long now," he says. "Hold on tight!"

The peaceful rhythmic sound of the river grows louder. A waterfall is nearby. Kharon doesn't turn us around or go in a different direction. No, we are heading straight for it.

"What are you doing?" I bellow, springing up to my feet. "Turn us around."

"Trust me. Down we go! But I told you to hold on!" he shouts.

Kharon grabs me by my arm right as we plunge downward. The incline is steep, and I am starved of air the faster we go. Somehow, we stay planted on the boat, and Kharon cracks a weird smile. I guess the look on my face tells him all.

With a loud plunk, we land below as if we were never falling off a waterfall. My head bobs back and forth in disbelief. The Underworld is not like our world at all. No part of it is the same. I see a sandy beach ahead and call out, "Land ahead."

When we dock, I stagger ashore on unsteady legs. But Clotho's image buoys my spirit. She believes in us. Now I must believe in her and get my strength back to aid her in her cause. Kharon docks the ferry but doesn't come to shore immediately. Instead, I see him sifting through crates and a chest.

"Ah-ha!" he exclaims, brandishing a dark amber bottle in his hands. "Here, drink this." He hands it over, and I stare up at him in bewilderment.

"Drink," he urges, pushing the bottle closer to my mouth.

"What is it?" I ask. I'll forever be cautious of drinks given to me after tangling with Carya the dryad.

"Do you wish to make haste?" he asks.

I don't hesitate to answer. "Why, yes, of course?"

"It will restore all your strength and then some. Better guzzle the entire bottle down." He takes the bottle, pops the cork off, and hands it back to me.

I glance down at the murky bottle clasped in my hands, then back up to meet Kharon's twinkling gaze. Clotho said he was her closest friend, so I decide to put my full trust in him, despite feeling as if I'm insane to do so.

Gripping the bottle's neck, I steel my nerves and throw back my head. Bitter liquid fire courses down my throat as I force myself to swallow mouthful after mouthful, fighting the urge to retch. The foul potion seems to curdle on my tongue, leaving behind an acrid film coating my entire mouth.

Within moments, the bottle is empty. Gasping, I lower it with a shudder, eyes watering from the vile taste still clinging to my gums and teeth.

A low chuckle croaks out beside me. I turn to see Kharon smiling wryly for a second, but then his look changes—part disdain, part grudging respect.

"Few mortals can drink my brew so readily. Count yourself lucky. You appear to possess something they do not." He extends his hand, long fingers curling around the bottle as I relinquish it with relief.

"Clotho's love is worth enduring far worse concoctions than that," I state, gritting my teeth as I will iron into my still-roiling stomach.

To my surprise, a gravelly chortle bubbles up from the Ferryman's wizened frame. His gaunt torso shakes as he emits a series of rasping laughs, a bizarre sound not meant to emanate from a dour immortal.

"Indeed, it would seem the little Fate has bewitched you proper, mortal!" Kharon wheezes out between hoarse cackles. "Only true devotion to her could compel such a sacrifice."

His ochre eyes peer at me shrewdly as mirth continues wavering in his tone. Wiping a grimy tear from his cheek, Kharon regards me with something akin to approval through the perpetual gloom underlying his expression. "Best hurry, then, and see what aid your devotion can offer against the likes of Cronos himself."

I look ahead at the fields of grass meeting the beach, and turn back, nodding. "And what of you? Will you stay here a bit longer? Do you wait or will you go?"

A faint smile tugs at his weathered lips. "My role is eternal transit. This is where our paths diverge. Beyond here lies your destiny."

"Thank you for everything. I've been truly blessed by those who are Clotho's truest friends."

Kharon's hand extends a reassuring grip. "You are welcome. I suggest you head out now. May your resolve serve you and your lady well with whatever lies ahead."

With a curt nod of thanks, I depart and head further inland. Kharon fades behind me, an enigmatic yet loyal guide through this trial's darkest stretch so far.

The landscape ahead is wrought with strange magic. As the soil swirls about, the sky undergoes a transformation, shifting through all the hours of a single day. Never have I witnessed such a clear night sky, where even the faintest constellations are visible. Aetheria's two moons light up the scenery around me, illuminating my path forward. I had no idea the Underworld shared the same sky.

Off in the distance lies an even stranger forest. Tall monoliths dot the barren land before the trees begin. I ready myself for anything. The work of the Titan's power is strong here. With each cautious step I take, the ground beneath me feels uncertain. The branches of the trees curl ominously toward me, clutching at me with thin, knobby fingers. Misshapen roots twist around the bases of the trunks, plunging into the ground, wrapping their way around the sides of the trail I walk.

There is a peculiar beauty about this place, one that draws me deeper into the woods and closer to Clotho. The murky forest swallows the last hints of light as I press deeper into the gloom. Between the trees are phantom souls in random scenes. In a moment of excitement, I spot Clotho and rush towards her, only to realize it's a bittersweet illusion of our shared memories.

What cruelty is this? A warp in time to torture me before we truly reunite. A sliver of unease slides icily down my back. There are more things to face before I reach her, I realize, and dread sets in. *What if I don't make it?* I shake the thought from my head. No, I will not give in to thoughts meant to deter me.

Wisps of mist slither through the trees, rolling in foul energies I do not wish to tangle with. I keep to the path but increase my pace. The faster I go, the more the forest groans and the memories of my family begin to haunt me on all sides.

I have long carried the burden of thinking their deaths were my fault, but my choices were limited. The king of our lands made it clear. Fight or die. I chose to live so they would not have to survive without me. Little did I know leaving my wife and daughter would mean I'd be living a life without them.

My wife, Cecilia, appears in front of me, holding my daughter Marcella. What trickery is this? They appear to me as they did the day I found them dead. Their blond hair tangles around their faces, bodies sunken in. Cronos appears to be the cruel Titan the Olympians claim him to be. To show a man the lifeless bodies of his wife and only child again. What sort of monster is he to do this? I can't bear to see the apparitions any longer, but something stirs about them, a soft glow pulses around their ever still forms.

Their weak and starved bodies begin to fill out, muscle and flesh blossoming on their withered frames. Cecilia's cheeks grow rosy and full as breath stirs in her lungs once more. Marcella's little body twitches next to hers and her big, curious eyes lock on mine. They seem alive and well. What is happening? My whole body shakes as little Marcella reaches out to me with her tiny hands. She mouths *Father*, and relief floods through me as I reach out to grab her, but something stays my hand. No, this feels wrong. They were dead; I know they were. I carried their bodies to graves I dug myself.

My throat tightens as I relive the day I put my beloveds in the ground. Tears roll down my cheeks. I scooped up their fragile bodies dressed in matching pale green dresses. I placed them together as I had found them and hugged their icy bodies, screaming to the gods to give them life again. I can see the clods of dirt on my hands still, knowing I would never hear their sweet voices again.

Whatever torture this is. It is more than I can bear as Marcella creeps closer. No, this is not real. “Stop this madness,” I plead.

She reaches out to me again and our hands meet, but mine passes through hers. A brutal reminder that they are not truly here. Cecilia approaches, and somehow her touch is real as she brushes her fingertips along my chin. Marcella rushes into my arms and hugs me. She is solid. This is real. They’re alive. This is not a dream. My mind tingles, and something tells me *no, you must go to Clotho*. But here they are, my family, and they wait for me to join them. Marcella tugs at my clothing, and they both beckon me to follow them deeper into the forest. But something is off; something doesn’t sit right with me.

I stay planted. My thoughts are confusing. Where am I? What was I doing? I want to go with Cecilia and Marcella, yet an unknown force stops me. I cannot go with them until I gain clarity.

Again, my family motions for me to follow. Before I can move, a bone-rattling roar shakes the forest. The very trees tremble and crack as the largest dog I’ve ever seen crashes through them. Branches bend and snap before tumbling to the ground. I stumble back, frozen in terror. Each slavering head of the massive beast is as large as a mountain lion.

This is Cerberus. The hellish hound that guards Hades's Underworld. Saliva drips from his gaping jaws. His hulking mass bounds toward me and I flinch, waiting for razor claws and sharp teeth to dig their way in. This is the end. But giant tongues loll out from each maw in a flurry of licking and excited yips—leaving a long, dripping trail of slobber down both arms and across my chest.

The beast's joy is like a puppy's, despite his imposing size. He lifts one head up, and the other two follow suit. A deep, guttural growl emits low from his belly and he snaps at my family. Confusion sets in and I place my hand up.

"Whoa, boy. Heel," I command. But his growls persist.

"Stop. This is my family."

Cerberus whines and cocks one head, peering in my direction before nudging my chest backward, pushing me away from my wife and child. That same snarl deep within him bellows out into a long, drawn-out howl.

Cecilia and Marcella cover their ears, their bodies trembling from the unholy sound emitting from each of Cerberus's heads.

"Dada, help!" Marcella screams.

I try to run to her, but Cerberus pounces on me and my back meets the earth with a thud. He woofs and stares in their direction. Marcella's plump cheeks sink in, Cecilia's arms twist and bend before shriveling so thin I can see bone beneath the flesh. Ashen, sallow skin replaces the glow of life that is within. Whatever light was there now diminishing. My wife and child are gone. They are nothing but husks of their former selves.

That is right! They have been dead for ten years! This is all a lie!

I spring up and back away from the shades. When I do, they rush over to me, but Cerberus stops them before they get any closer with a loud bark that sends them cowering low to the ground. The specters of my family let out wails so shrill I clutch my head as the noise shatters branches off the trees surrounding us, piercing my ears with their soul-rending cry.

Cerberus lets out a distressed bellow to match their screams, pawing the earth and snapping his powerful jaws at their intangible souls. Blood pounds in my skull, drowning out all thought besides the urgent need to flee this place.

Shuddering, I tear my eyes from the visions persisting with their blood-curdling screeching.

"Stop this! I cannot take this torment," I beg, clutching my ears.

"P-Please. I can't take much more pleas–"

Their phantasmal glare meets mine one last time. "Ares, please stop this madness if you have the power to."

Their cries fade into a distant, hopeless sobbing. Gripped by grief and terror, I'm nailed in place as Marcella's and Cecilia's bodies disintegrate to ash in front of me. I realize my cheeks are wet with tears. The pain persists, and I fall to my knees. This sorrow, this insanity, is more than I can take. But Cerberus, by some grace, is here to assist me. The three-headed beast nudges me gently, and I press my hands deep into his black fur.

A calmness overcomes my rattled psyche and resolve steadies my mind. I must go forward. I must go to Clotho. I rise and leave the nightmares behind, with Cerberus looming protectively nearby. The trials I've endured have pushed me to the brink. This last one nearly broke my soul in two. I would have battled the Styx's wraiths for eternity rather than suffer the torment of losing my family again.

The sobbing doesn't cease behind me despite their bodies being gone, but my mind is my own, and I bid my family's souls goodbye one last time. While they are lost to me now, they are not forgotten. Two things can remain true. I will always hold love for them, and I can love Clotho, too.

26

The Clock Ticks

Marcellus

The forest gives way to a strange barren field of dirt mounds. Shriveled bodies of creatures I've never seen lay strewn about. Whatever they were, something mangled most of the bodies beyond recognition. But some remind me of the goblins of Zaros—with their grayish skin and twisted limbs. I take my next steps slowly, as I am not sure what to expect next. Cerberus's fur ripples and sticks straight up as the energy shifts around us. I scan the path ahead for any movement when a metallic glimmer catches my eye. I glance down, spying the hilt of a short sword peeking out from one of the fallen beast's hips, and crouch low, easing the body to the side.

The imp's hollow eyes stare past me as I wrest the blade from its rigid grip. I stand, testing the sword's weight and give it a good swing. *This will do and beats having to use only my dagger.* With a steading breath, I stride forward and prepare to defend myself if need be. I am ready for anything, or so I think...

In an instant, the mounds in front of us shift back and forth, growing bigger than they were before. The dirt of one erupts upwards, spewing forth the ugliest little brute I've ever seen. He bares his teeth and grunts before charging. His bulging eyes locking on mine before letting out a screech that chills me to the bone. Cerberus howls and rushes toward him. His sharp teeth sink deep into the little demon's torso before he shakes it about like a rag doll.

More mounds explode with these creatures popping up, and my mouth gapes open. What the hell is happening now? Endless imps spring out, their piercing screeches drilling into my ears, radiating agony throughout my skull. I've never seen these vermin in my life. This is gods' magic, utter madness. What sickness of the mind holds some immortals this tight, that they'd torture me and Clotho for the love we have?

What other form of purity is there? Why these punishments over the one thing that makes Aetheria better? I can't make sense of it, but I raise my sword and cut the tiny gnats down with focused strikes. There is no time for distractions. I must keep moving forward no matter the costs. I steel myself against the horrors ahead, determined to overcome what I hope is the final trial.

What else could these experiences be? We left the farm and an onslaught of adversity has followed.

I'm tired of tests, first Minos, then those nymphs, the distorted time, those damned souls after mine. Then my family. I am ready for this all to end. I howl out a war cry, and Cerberus follows. The three-headed hound is not my Maximus, but I appreciate his presence and abilities. We weave through the grotesque horde with great speed, cutting them down with ease. As we do this, I hear the low tones of a clock ticking, ticking. *Not this again. The beating flesh pod was enough!* I drown out the disorder surrounding me with one goal in mind: reach Clotho before time runs out. The eerie ticking reverberates like a countdown in my mind, driving me to push ahead.

I can only surmise that the clock is there to remind me how close I am to failing.

The creatures keep popping up by the dozen; droves of those beastly demons come for us. Cerberus scoops me up in his mouth like I'm his pup and sprints faster than I could ever run. He tosses me up in the air next, and I see myself flying over his head. I plunk right down on his back and hold on. That damned clock is still ticking, and those little fiends still pursue me, their constant shrieking fraying the edges of my sanity.

The discordant clamor of the imps' weapons and battle cries gets louder with each second. I swear my luck has been godlike. If it were just me facing off against these puny devils, I'd be running for my life.

The barren landscape gives way, and up ahead, I see a glowing hill. Is this where Clotho and Cronos are? Cerberus is heading right for it. It must be. I am elated and ready to reunite with my love.

The clock is ticking faster. The gremlins nip closely at our heels. Time is running out. *No, we will make it!* Our love is forbidden in words only. It transcends the ages. It is infinite. I have faith; I have hope.

The clock ticks....

The aura emitting from the mountain is closer....

My heart thuds hard against my chest in time with Cerberus's run. The mouth of a cavern comes into view. We are so close now, but I see the opening shrinking. Cerberus slides to the entrance in one last effort to get me to my destination.

I slink off his back, thank him, and dive in before the mouth closes. The walls around me are caving in. I run fast, my feet pounding hard into the ground. The way I came is closing in. I have no choice but to go forward. I call out to Cerberus, but he is too large to come with me. "Thank you. I promise we will meet again!"

I can sense Clotho's energy, and I push off into a sprint. The quietness of the passageway threatens to crush my very being. I try to look on the bright side of things—at least the ticking is gone, and I must be close to the end. My limbs shake the more I travel inward to Cronos's domain.

Two voices shatter the stillness as they converse ahead. I recognize one—*Clotho*—my heart lurches as I bolt toward the opening. I watch in horror as the edges constrict and begin to seal shut. I push my aching legs faster, my pulse thrashing as desperation fuels every step. I'm mere steps away when the entry threatens to pinch off completely. I hurl myself into the silvery portal, slipping into an enormous cavern that is both haunting and beautiful.

A giant of a man on a tangled root throne contrasts the shimmering sides of the cavern. Next to him is Clotho, and part of me can't believe my eyes. There she is, how I have missed her, her golden locks, her smile. Clotho's entire countenance fills me with happiness. I am home, and a sense of ease overcomes me. My gaze locks with hers and I run to her side. I gather her up in my arms and see tears form in her eyes. A whirlwind of emotions and kisses blocks out everything else. With every touch of her lips on mine, I am reminded of why I endured and why I will continue to fight. I will do anything to keep her by my side.

Maximus whines, and I rub the top of his head. "I missed you, boy." He licks my hand, and I keep one arm dangling to give him all the scratches he deserves.

A thunderous voice fills my ears next. "Ah, the mortal, Marcellus. You're lucky you made it."

I glance over at the colossal being of mass proportions. I am confused by the pleasant tone in his voice. I thought for sure we'd be facing some sort of test from him. But we all stand here. A wry smile forms on his face as Clotho takes my hand in hers.

"Do I have your promise, Titan of old?" she asks.

Cronos grins slyly. "As long as you're prepared to keep your side of the bargain."

"I am," she says, dipping her chin down to convey their agreement.

I am confused. What has transpired between them, and what is the plan?

"Your mortal is curious about our dealings. I'd suggest keeping the details to a minimum, as his mind may not be as protected as you and your siblings." Cronos cracks his neck.

This is a surprising turn of events. One side of Cronos's face is distorted while the other remains unchanged, so it is hard to read his true intentions. The one eye I can focus on peers down at me with intense scrutiny.

"Are we free to leave?" she asks next.

"Yes. When Zeus summons you to the Mounts, be ready. Until then, I offer this as a gift. No god or person otherwise will interfere until you are called to talk to my son."

Before I can speak or respond, darkness consumes my view as the Titan fades off into the distance. Within seconds, we are back in my house. Confusion washes over me again. I am curious about Clotho and Cronos's deal and what they have planned next.

Clotho squeals and hugs me tight. Maximus entangles himself around our legs. I take the time to truly reunite with them, but a question lingers in my mind. "What deal did you agree to?" I finally ask.

"One that ensures we get to be together, but Zeus is notorious for not keeping his word. In this case, my siblings and I have a way to force him to do what is right."

Something doesn't sit right with me. Forcing his hand; this can't be good. "What word do you think he'll break?" I wish she could share more. Is this related to Cronos warping time or something else?

"Cronos is right. I cannot divulge all the details, as your mind is not protected. Can you put your trust in my siblings? Can you continue to trust me?" She bites her lip, and I can sense she is worried I won't.

I try to comfort her unease. "I trust you, but is this regarding us or Cronos himself?"

"I cannot say."

"Us?" I ask.

She shakes her head.

"Cronos?"

She stares into my eyes, barely nodding, and I accept that answer. Part of me wants her to tell me more, but when we thought Zeus was clueless, he had already set in motion the tests placed upon us. Now is the time to tread with care.

"Do you know when he will call for us?" I question.

"No, but Cronos offered me something."

"Offered what?"

"Time together."

She pulls me close to her, and I must ask one more thing. "How much time?"

"Enough that we can fully enjoy being reunited as one before the summons." She tugs me even closer. Her body presses against mine, and I melt as she caresses my arms. My body responds to her every touch.

I gaze into her eyes, searching. "Does this feel right, my heart?" I ask, my voice but a whisper. "I won't pressure or rush you."

A soft smile crosses her face. "It does. There is no one else I'd rather share this with."

I cup her face with utmost tenderness and let my thumb caress her flushed cheeks. "Let us savor being together in peace and see where our passion leads us, my lady."

She leans into my palm and covers my hand with her own. "I love you," she breathes.

"And I love you," I rasp, crushing my mouth onto hers. Her lips part and I delve inside, my tongue swirling and stroking as she trembles in my arms.

She threads her fingers through my hair as she moans into our kiss. "Being with you has always felt so right."

The feeling is mutual. Desire rages through my veins like never before. "I feel the same."

I trail kisses along her jawline as I continue exploring her delicate skin. Whispering in her ear, I tell her, "Tell me what you want, and if anything displeases you, I'll stop, my love." Our fingers entwine with an irresistible pull, and a soft whimper escapes her lips as my palm grazes over her ample breasts.

I rid myself of my shirt and assist Clotho out of her dress. My breath hitches as she stands before me in all her ethereal glory. I commit each feature to memory—her tumbling waves of golden blond hair, her petal-soft skin like creamy porcelain. My gaze travels over her graceful curves, all gentle slopes and swells I long to explore. As I stare at her face, her enchanting aquamarine eyes consume me entirely. I cup her buttocks and scoop her up in my arms, eliciting a surprise gasp from her. She wraps her legs around my waist as I carry her to our bed.

I lean her back and glide my fingers down her stomach to her luscious core. One of her hands pushes on mine as I slowly stroke my thumb on her clit while a finger slips inside. With each undulating motion, her back arches with pleasure, and she moans my name. A sweet symphony that only stokes the flames of the want growing within me.

She ushers me up to her chest, my hard cock pressing on her opening. Her body melds against mine as her eyes flicker with a sense of urgency. I lick my finger. She tastes so sweet, like the nectar of the gods. The bed creaks under our weight as we align perfectly together. I can feel her body's response to me, the way she clenches her legs around me, and how wet she is. I can't tear my gaze from hers. Still mesmerized by the captivating depth of those enchanting eyes, I lock in and rock my lower half against hers. My heart beats like a drum.

She presses her body into mine and I press back. "Are you sure you want this?"

"Please," she says breathlessly.

Our lips meet, and I tenderly kiss her until she responds eagerly, pressing into me as our mouths urgently intertwine. Soon, we lose control. She rubs against me, and her wetness threatens to undo me. I whisper, "Are you ready?" and she nods. It is all I can do not to lose it as I kiss down her collarbone and take one nipple in my mouth. Sucking hard, I slam into her with my length. Her back arches, and soft moans roll out from her lips.

"M–Marcellus," she gasps as I slide my cock out and slam back in, harder and further into her until I am lost in all of her, her beauty, her soul in the way she moves and cries out with each thrust.

Our skin slides against each other in a symphony of moans and pleasure, our hearts racing in tandem. I kiss her as we rock together. My free hand explores her breasts again, tweaking her nipples gently before moving down and playing with her clit more.

Her scent surrounds me, intoxicating and addictive. "Gods!" she cries. I feel her tense around me as her moans become louder, and my cock hardens to almost painful limits as she pulses around me. I watch her come undone, and I follow. I cry out her name and as it spills from my lips I spill inside her. I pull out and stare down at her, watching as her expression melts into contentment and satisfaction.

Her nipples remain puckered and red, begging for me to kiss them, so I do. I trail kisses along her stomach, traveling down to her clit as she watches me in half-lidded bliss. When I lick her, she quivers. "What are you doing?"

"I'm not finished with you. Before the night is done, you will shake with pleasure. That I can promise you."

Clotho

Marcellus spreads my lips and slips his fingers in, moving them in and out as his tongue swirls across my clit. I begin to convulse in waves of pleasure. My legs quiver between each quick breath, and I am lost in his touch. With each gasp and each pulse of his fingers, he sends me spiraling further. As his fingers leave my body, he begins a tantalizing exploration, tracing his lips, tongue, and hands over every inch of me. I beg him to finish me.

I can feel his hard length again, and I breathlessly say, "You mean to go again?"

He smirks. "What did I promise?" With a slow, deliberate push, he penetrates me inch by inch. The sensation is unlike anything I've ever felt, and my body aches for more. My legs are almost jelly, my head swimming in unadulterated ecstasy. Our bodies move in perfect sync, riding the waves of pleasure together. I rake my nails across his back as our passion escalates into something wild, each thrust building until we both unravel.

27

Reunited

Clotho

Our bodies shudder in unison as we come off our high. His cries of satisfaction magnify my own. Marcellus slowly pulls out and lies beside me on the bed. Time seems to stand still as we lay there, our bodies intertwined, catching our breath and basking in the afterglow of lovemaking.

He wraps his arms around me, and he whispers into my ear, "I love you."

"I love you, too," I reply, still panting, as I snuggle deeper into his embrace. In that moment, I know this is exactly where I belong—in Marcellus's arms forever.

We lay there, simply enjoying each other's company as Marcellus traces delicate caresses over my arm, shoulders, and back, pressing gentle kisses to my temple as our heartbeats slow in sync. We revel in the farm's tranquility. I missed these nights, where the songs of crickets are the only things to be heard.

I glide my hands over his strong arms and prop up on the pillow. I gently caress his face and run my fingers through his hair, kissing his forehead. He gazes up at me, his eyes shining. "When this is all over, I want to build a life together," I whisper.

Marcellus sits up, taking my hands in his. "We will make it work. You can spin threads no matter what or where you are. We can divide our time between the farm and the Mounts.

I pull him into a kiss, happiness bubbling up inside me. In all my immortal life, I never dared to dream of a future filled with such bliss. Yet now with Marcellus I sense this possibility, and I want it.

"Yes, my love, I think we can do that," I say, returning his smile. As long as we are together, any life we create will be perfect in my eyes.

Marcellus gets out of bed and stretches. Turning to me, he says, "Wait here. Oh, and when I come back, close those eyes!"

I hear his footsteps travel across the house and clanking of metal next. The sound of water being pumped lightly echoes into the bedroom and I wonder what he is up to. I hear him talking softly to Maximus next before I spot him coming back to the room.

"Ready?" he asks.

"Yes."

"Close your eyes." I pinch my eyes shut and he takes my hand.

He guides me out of the bedroom and across the house. "You can look now," he says.

My lids flutter open. We are in the washroom and Marcellus has prepared a hot bath. Lit candles surround the tub, and there are fresh towels on a stool for us. Marcellus helps me into the water and slides in behind me. He tenderly washes my back, massaging the soap and warmth into my tired muscles. I bask in the comforting heat of the water and his ever-gentle touch.

I return the care he gives me and wash him next, taking my time with each stroke across his muscled back. I soap up his chest and travel downward, taking my time to learn his body like he has learned mine. He tilts his head back and relaxes. I sit between his legs and rest against him now.

We take our time in the bath, then dry off and put fresh clothes on. He holds my hand and guides me to the kitchen. There isn't much there besides dried fruits and nuts. Marcellus places some in a bowl, and we dig right in.

The amount of food may be small, but I savor each bite, as I know the work he puts into everything he has. Tomorrow, I am sure Zeus will summon us to the Mounts, and I am ready to deal with him. I don't focus on these thoughts much, instead returning them back to my love. Because tonight is special, and my focus should be on him.

Every moment is truly ours. I am grateful for an old Titan who saw to that.

28

Anticipation

Clotho

Four days pass, and there is no word from Zeus. He is not one to wait and often chooses swift action over mindful deliberation. I am surprised he didn't summon us the very moment Cronos returned to the portal entrance of Tartarus. Every passing hour feels like an eternity of waiting. I am curious if I can truly live without worrying about what Zeus will do next. I want to know if I can be with Marcellus without further assault. Despite my efforts to stay level-headed, the wait is becoming almost unbearable to deal with. My stomach twists itself into knots as I wring my hands in my lap. I cannot rein in this nervous energy. What ifs plague my waking thoughts and nightmarish images invade my dreams.

Marcellus senses my growing unease and pulls me to his side of the bed, his arms wrapping around me in a warm, comforting embrace. His steady breathing and the beat of his heart against mine help bring my racing pulse back down. *Why is this taking so long?* I know I should brush aside the tension I'm feeling and enjoy the extra time, but what could Zeus be deliberating?

We get up and head to the kitchen together. The anxiety continues to poke and prod me at the edges of my mind. *What if Zeus makes the Mount we live on a literal prison my sisters and I cannot escape? What if he kills Marcellus?* All I can do is try shutting down each new horrible thought that crops up.

The continued silence from the god-king is deafening. I try to distract myself by working alongside Marcellus in the garden after breakfast. The warm sun beats down on us as we dig up the earth, preparing small holes for new seeds to sprout up. Maximus trots behind us, tail wagging and tongue lolling, as we drop one seedling in each little pit for the next harvest of radishes.

Spring is in full force, and according to Phoebe, only a week has passed since we left for our journey, but she mentions many things that concern me. "The skies behaved so oddly these past few days. As I gazed upon the heavens, the blanket of stars shifted within seconds and the night became day. New constellations appeared. Even stranger are the tales of new creatures popping out of the earth. Some were small and twisted. Others large with eyes like firepits and their skin like hardening lava rocks."

My heart leaps out of my chest. What I did had rippling consequences, just as Pythia had said.

Alexius clears his throat, taking a step closer to Marcellus and me. In his ever-solemn tone, he says, "Let us not forget to mention the news of tremors cracking the earth wide open in distant lands off the shores of Aetheria. Places that have never seen a single quake suddenly rattled relentlessly by seismic forces."

Guilt overcomes me as I realize what combining our threads did to the entire continent. I almost lose myself in thought when I hear Alexius and Marcellus calling out my name.

"Clotho, are you okay?"

"Yes, sorry."

"Your breathing changed. Are you sure you are all right?" Marcellus asks.

"It is nothing. I... I hope the people of Aetheria will be all right."

Phoebe reaches for me and squeezes my hand. "We are a tough lot. From Roma to Grecia and beyond. Aetheria picks itself up after disasters and moves along right away."

I know she speaks of human will. But any harm that has fallen on the people is my fault. Pythia warned me and warned me well. I knew to take heed. Yet I stare at Marcellus and know I have found the other half to my soul.

And all seems to be set right, for now. But I worry. What really happened when I set in motion the events that played out? Sure, Marcellus and I had our tests, but I still can't make sense of what happened during our trials. Time appeared to twist and turn, causing days to pass quickly and moments to feel everlasting. Marcellus, who eluded Minos for a day before fleeing to the sea, acknowledges how quickly it all seemed to occur, but it also felt like eternity.

Maybe we'll never fully understand what happened, but we can be sure of one thing: we didn't give up despite all the challenges we faced. Still, a small part of me fears Zeus may go back on his word once I present him with the deal I struck. But he never explicitly forbade such a promise. My siblings are ready when I need them, and this may be the move that changes everything for immortals and mortals alike. Marcellus and I are but one couple of many who have been told we cannot have our love. I hope our trials help others on similar pathways in the future to come.

Atropos and Lachesis want to visit, and I eagerly say yes. My chest flutters a bit, so much has happened, but I am elated to see my sisters in the next few hours. We have weathered so much together. They have been at my side through thick and thin. Although I may be the most nurturing, they have always looked out for me. When our mother and other siblings were banished to Tartarus by Zeus, they saw me through that painful separation.

Even though they were not with me as I faced Cronos, they lent me their energies, too. I picture Atropos's gentle smile and Lachesis's wise eyes as Marcellus and I prepare the guest room in his farmhouse.

I smooth the hand-stitched quilt on the bed, recalling the daughter that once slept here. "Thank you for opening your home to my sisters. I know this room is sacred to you."

Marcellus squeezes my hand. A bittersweet smile is on his lips. "Of course, my heart. Your family is now my family, too. I want to make sure they feel welcomed to our humble abode."

My heart swells, and I pull him into an embrace. No matter how many times he shows his innate kindness, I am always blown away by it.

Later, as we whip up lunch, I confide in Marcellus about my brother, Thanatos. My sisters and I asked him to tag along, but he declined. "I wish Thanatos would visit too, but he insists on waiting until we confront Zeus," I tell him.

Marcellus's brow furrows. "Did he tell you why?"

"He said there are shadow entities watching him closely. They have blamed him for your thread going missing, although I am the one who took it." I sigh, regret gnaws at me. If only we could all be together without further assault, truly free from Zeus's prodding energies.

Marcellus gives my shoulders a reassuring squeeze. "We will set things right. Patience, my love, the time will come, and I know we will be free."

"I hope so. Let us not underestimate the god-king."

"Never," he says.

I go to set the table when a familiar voice echoes in my mind. "Little sister, we're almost there!" Atropos's excitement is palpable, her words so clear as if she were standing right beside me. I spring to the front door.

"My sisters are close." I beam.

"Let us meet them outside, then." Marcellus is right behind me as I creak the door open. We walk hand in hand toward the road and I spot my sisters; they are running toward us from the thick trees, and I squeal, sprinting to meet them and tugging Marcellus along. The sight of them fills me with a sense of comfort and belonging that I have missed deeply during our trials.

"Clotho!" they both shout.

Tears well up in my eyes, and we hug each other all at once.

"I missed you both," I say.

"What a thing you've been through, my sister." Lachesis hugs me tight.

Atropos just stares at me. Something in her eyes makes me think something is the matter. "Is everything all right, my sister?" I ask.

"Everything is perfect. Yet, you have changed. And dare I say, I love it!" she squeaks before pulling me into the deepest hug she's ever given me.

"And this is the mortal man that has captivated our sister's heart?" Lachesis asks next.

I grab Marcellus's hand, nodding, but guilt pricks every part of me. "Yes, this is Marcellus. Forgive me for not confiding in both of you."

"Oh, sister, no apologies needed. Long have we watched you suffer in your loneliness, seen you joyless for far too many years, and right now, you're positively glowing! We only wish for your happiness, and we are glad you found it." Lachesis embraces me, and Atropos nods in hearty agreement.

"It is a pleasure to meet you, Marcellus," Atropos says.

Lachesis chimes in. "Yes, agreed."

Atropos smiles as Marcellus steps forward. He is the epitome of gentlemanly charm, taking her slender hand into his and bowing. He turns to Lachesis and clasps her outstretched palm next, placing a chaste kiss on her knuckles. "The pleasure is all mine, ladies."

Atropos's cheeks flush a little and Lachesis titters. He has endeared both with his amiability. I can't help but grin in response.

A blur of silvery fur suddenly barrels around the farmhouse. Maximus makes straight for Atropos, burying his great head beneath her skirts. She startles, flustered by the brazen hound nosing at her dress, but as soon as she glances down and sees his sweet honeyed-brown eyes, she melts. Atropos sinks her fingers into his fur, stroking his head and all tension dissipates under his affectionate gaze.

"Maximus, it seems you have made a new friend." Marcellus laughs.

My sister smiles, her initial alarm fading as Maximus runs his head and torso along her legs.

"That he has. What a regal and sweet boy you have here," she says.

Marcellus winks at me, amusement dancing in his eyes. Maximus approaches Lachesis slowly and gently nudges her side. His gaze settles on her, and he waits. She looks down and gives him a solid pat and rubs his ears next. "An intelligent beast at that," she remarks.

"Yes, dare I say, too smart for his own good most of the time." Marcellus chuckles as his faithful companion emits a low growl and edges toward him. Marcellus crouches and Maximus playfully nips his wrist before bounding back toward the farm.

"He has the right idea. Shall we proceed to the house? Clotho and I prepared lunch for everyone."

Marcellus takes my arm into his and motions for my sisters to follow. All of us head into the house. My sisters gasp in unison when they see the table: Fresh baked bread, soft cheeses, roasted vegetables, and cured meat with olives fill up a large wooden platter. Two carafes of Marcellus's mulled wine are on either side.

"Come sit, let's eat," I say, guiding them both to their seats.

Lachesis takes to the cheese, and Atropos grabs several slices of bread. I wait for them to take the first bites before filling my plate.

"This bread is divine!" Atropos takes an enthusiastic bite, melting into her chair further.

"Mmm, this is so delicious!" Lachesis sighs blissfully. "Who made all of this?"

"Marcellus and me." I beam.

"Wow, your cooking is glorious on its own, dear sister, but with the two of you combined, I am sincerely captivated. It may seem simple, but the flavors are astounding," Lachesis praises between bites.

Marcellus fills our wine cups and says, "Thank you," before sitting down next to me.

"Yes, thank you. I must know, what news do you bring from the Mounts?" I ask, curious about what is happening above us as we speak.

Lachesis smooths out her napkin as she talks. "Zeus is in counsel with the other eleven. Most are in your favor, but I don't trust him. No one does. We all thought Cronos a monstrosity, but you convinced him to retreat without more of our world being torn asunder. The mortals do not even seem to be aware of what was befalling them."

I can't help but feel a twinge of anxiety at her words. Despite my success in convincing Cronos to retreat without causing too much destruction, I am still haunted by the cost of my bargain. "Do you still believe our plan is worth it?"

Atropos speaks up, surprising me with her determination. "Yes, a thousand times over, dear Sister."

That is all I need to hear to know they would never betray me. I questioned it in the Underworld for a split second. It was a lot to ask. Yet here they are. They showed up and are ready to do what needs to be done when the time comes.

This is all I need to know. Our family sticking together when it matters most.

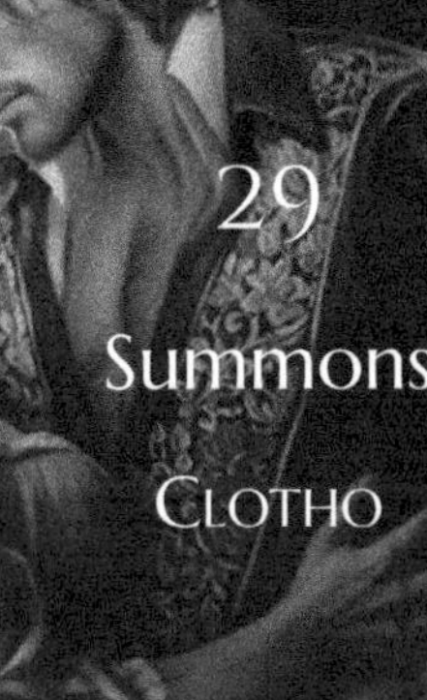

29

Summons

Clotho

Twilight is upon us, and Zeus has summoned us to the Mounts today. His message came to me while I slept, jolting me awake. Anxiety pools in my belly, spreading out into my limbs. My nerves are alight and predicting the worst. I know the god-king will not favor the promise I made to Cronos back in that cave, but my choice was made, and Marcellus and I have come out on the other side of the tests alive. While not wholly unscathed, we got through them. We proved our love is true.

Zeus is bound by his words in that regard, yet I know he will push against Cronos ruling Tartarus. Contrary to what I thought, Zeus holds on to the past he shares with his father instead of becoming a beacon of hope and peace.

I can't pretend to comprehend Zeus's motives. I hold a certain optimism that he will see things as I do: give the mad Titan the thing he desires. If he missteps, we deal with it right away with certain conditions in place. I will personally be in the frontlines to stop his ascent if he proves to be a liar.

Maybe I am making it out to be easier than it sounds. But in his bid to protect Aetheria, Zeus has become much of the tyrant his father once was. I suspect Cronos is now in a humbler state. If he was truly as terrible as they have made him out to be, why did he gift me such precious time with Marcellus? He gains nothing from it. In this case, I must trust my intuition and proceed with the plan, and, if necessary, fight more for the love I share with Marcellus, and for those gods and mortals who wish to love freely as well.

I cannot undo what has been done. There is one more thing to do, and it's facing the last test. The one where I must stand my ground when facing Zeus.

As I nervously move around the kitchen. My sisters are watching my every move. Their eyes are upon me, eager for me to speak. Lachesis breaks the silence.

"Share your thoughts with us. Your pacing is driving me into madness."

I stop and turn to face her. "What if Zeus doesn't agree with our plan? What does it mean for all of us?"

Lachesis responds in a measured tone, "We already discussed this earlier. We all agreed this is the best course of action."

"It... it feels like a plan steeped in desperation," I say.

Lachesis crosses her arms and straightens her shoulders, "Zeus needs to be brought down a few notches. He doesn't see what most already do."

Atropos nods. "Lachesis is right. Let's refrain from speaking about this anymore, in case there are unseen observers peeking in on us. We need this to work, no surprises." Her eyes dart around the room. I agree. Everything we've planned has been in secret for many reasons.

"You've each made fair points. To rid myself of this worry, I need to have total faith in the plans we have made. I must wholeheartedly believe in the bond Marcellus and I share. I must lean on the strength of our family, knowing it will sustain. Surely, these things will be enough to steer us through until the very end."

I inhale deeply and allow the words to settle within me.

"Either way," I continue with determination, "we must move forward and stand firm when facing Zeus."

Lachesis gives me a reassuring pat on the back, and Atropos takes hold of my hand.

"We travel to the Mounts soon," Lachesis says, taking me into a quick hug. "I can see the sun peeping over the horizon. Go to Marcellus and enjoy your time before the final test."

She is always so calm while I fight the storm brewing inside me. The sun begins its ascent, and I head back into the bedroom with Marcellus. He lies there with the blankets around his waist, and I watch his chest rise and fall with each cherished breath he takes.

I climb back into the bed and nestle into the crook of his shoulder, breathing in his earthy scent. His strong arms encircle me, and I sink into the warmth of his body. I wish it were possible to stay here like this forever.

30

The Floating Mounts

Clotho

The five of us set out under a sky flecked with puffy, drifting clouds, following the well-worn roadways that wind through the uneven terrain marking the Roma-Greca border. Though the route is straightforward, the climb ahead promises to test anyone who dares to make it. Many travelers avoid the journey, content to admire the views from a safe distance.

As we ascend, the winding trail that leads us up narrows in places with crumbling stone edges. There are steep drop-offs guarded by nothing but tiny shrubs that couldn't save a mortal if they slipped. With each labored breath, the air grows thinner, and the temperature cools dramatically the higher we climb.

Wisps of clouds envelop us next, momentarily obscuring the landscape. My sisters and I tread lightly so as not to disturb mountain flowers, stubbornly taking root in cracks between stones. The birds in the sky appear as tiny specks against the expansive backdrop. They weave in and out of the mists of the mountaintops, their songs loud enough for us to hear.

Coming around a twisting bend, the wispy veils of cloud part to reveal a lush canyon far below, its depths vibrant with color. Sunlight dances upon forest and water in a rippling tapestry of emeralds and sapphires. Beside me, Marcellus gasps, captivated by the sheer grandeur of it all. My thumb rubs a small circle on his wrist in reassurance as his gaze follows the canyon's gorge to the horizon.

Ahead, the hazy shroud lifts to unveil the legendary Twelve Peaks of shimmering Olympus embedded within swirling mists. Marcellus freezes, transfixed by the sight of those soaring pinnacles that have captured imaginations for millennia. The pulse of mystical energies stirs as we draw ever closer to the home of the gods.

Our destination awaits just beyond, suspended between Heaven and Earth. Narrow walkways made of thick rope and sturdy wooden slabs connect to each floating platform from the center of the land we stand on. They fan out to each peak like the strings of a spider web.

Marcellus takes my arm. "I've heard the stories of the peaks, but this ... I have no words."

"It is captivating, isn't it? Are you excited to see the city of the gods?" I ask.

"I think I am, despite the reason." He chuckles. "Are there a lot of mortals here?"

"Yes, there are countless mortals who travel here to prove themselves to their chosen gods or goddesses. There are lines outside the temples. Some come to sell their wares and services. Others come seeking the Oracle, as Zeus does not forbid humans from seeking wisdom, if you can even call it that." I know my words sound bitter. The old crone was not wrong, but she wasn't right, either. Unless Pythia saw more of the future than she let on.

It wouldn't surprise me at this point. Some say she is older than the Titans, and others say she is an incarnation of her former self. Still ... I know that, in a way, her warning helped me come to terms with many things. Hiding on the Mounts didn't serve me well, and I knew what I was doing when I mixed my thread with Marcellus's.

Still, I wouldn't alter a single moment. The journey was worth it. I'd repeat the process even if I knew the outcome beforehand. I guess that is the oracle's true gift. The choices are mine to make, even when destiny is at play.

Marcellus squeezes my hand as we make our way across the largest platform in the center. This heads right to Zeus's palace. I manage to inhale and hold a deep breath, one that soothes my worry and steels me for the walk we are about to make.

This bridge is the sturdier of the other eleven, but the wind constantly whips through the thick cords that hold it together. Despite its strength compared to the other eleven, there is still a sense of unease as it sways and creaks under our weight. Though they are not visible, below are jagged peaks that spell death for any mortal and unimaginable pain for someone like myself.

Above us, dark clouds gather and mass together above the towering walls of our destination. A deep rumbling thunder echoes through the pass, making the planks beneath our feet shudder. Lightning strikes at the far end of the bridge; Zeus is exerting his power and wants Marcellus to feel it before we even get there.

As we draw closer to the city itself, I can't shake the feeling of unseen eyes watching us. I have no doubts in my mind that Zeus has riled up the immortals who want purity over progress. But I know there are many on my side, and I remain standing tall despite Zeus's wrath hovering over us now.

Maximus positions himself in front of me and Marcellus. His protective stance speaks volumes about the animosity surging around us. The tension gets thicker, like the fog blanketed below. Even my sisters seem to be affected, their usually cheerful spirits replaced by a somber tone.

But I refuse to let this negative energy taint my own. Cronos's was far worse. I glance at Marcellus and see that he, too, remains unfazed, perhaps due to our shared experiences or our recent reunion. Or both.

Our determination and love will not falter, even in the face of powerful opposition.

We reach the other side of the passage; the atmosphere is thick and charged. An electrical tension raises the small hairs on my arms. The glittering marble gates of the city are wide open, and the god-king awaits our arrival.

As we enter, an oppressive weight hangs over everything. The often loud and bustling streets are still busy, but there is an unnatural quiet that's taken hold. Hushed conversations reach my ears, and I know they are all aware of who we are. Immortals and mortals alike gather around the edges of the street.

Their eyes are all on us while we make our way to the palace. Zeus knows I hate undue attention drawn to me. He did this on purpose, to further apply the pressure he's put on me. He's never quite taken the Fates' station seriously. I cannot wait to show him what we are made of and just how strong true love is.

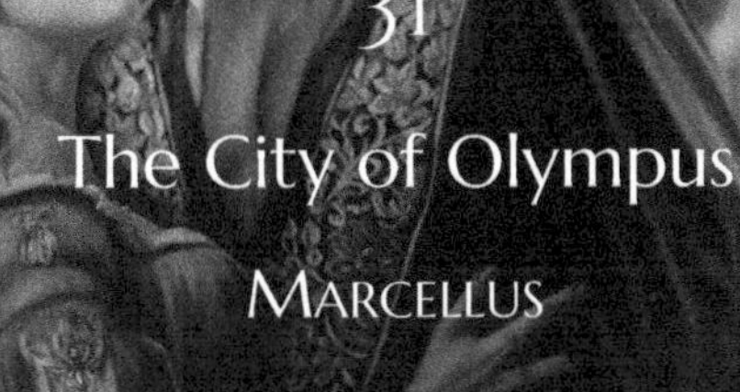

31

The City of Olympus

Marcellus

Clotho's hold tightens on my arm as we approach two majestic winged statues on each side of the gated entrance. Their stone eyes seem to follow us as we enter. The sunlight makes the marbled carvings on buildings shimmer. I always dreamed of coming here to speak with Ares. Now that I am here for different reasons, I wonder if it's still a possibility. I will have to wait and see what happens once we converse with Zeus. If time permits, I'd like to.

Dense energies press upon me. I try to remain calm. I am trusting my love's plan and following her next move. I hold no doubts that we will walk away from this place unscathed.

I notice all eyes are on us as we descend further into the marketplace. The golden stalls and white marbled tables make the entire area appear ethereal. Almost like a dream.

The people here seem at ease despite the gods and goddesses in their midst. I see a mortal shopkeeper haggling with an immortal, unphased by their towering presence. Children play in the streets, unbothered by the gods roaming around them. One of them even asks an immortal I am unfamiliar with to play tag. They have become accustomed to being amongst the gods day in and day out—a stark contrast to life in Aetheria where the immortals are venerated. I must be the only one here filled with unease as I walk among legends. My eyes drifting to each immortal face. I spot Hermes in an open shop. His features darken, and I look away. Not a single friendly face to be seen besides the company alongside me.

I wonder if they are all against us. Upsetting the balance is no small thing, yet I do not regret talking to Clotho the night we met. The moment our eyes locked, I knew we'd have a meaningful bond, and I had an instant desire to introduce myself to her.

As the night carried on, I knew my place was by her side, and the pain I felt during our separations was great. I never want to endure it again. They will have to rip us apart at the root of our souls, and even then, I'd fight on.

We continue forward, steadfast in our resolve. I glance over to Lachesis and Atropos and smile. For years, I've been living in solitude, without the comforting presence of family. From the moment we met, they wholeheartedly accepted me, and I am glad they walk with us now.

I try to think of what needs to be done on my end, but Clotho assures me I have completed what is required. We shall see. I do not know the gods personally as she does. I've only ever trusted in one, because he helped me many years ago when I was new to the battlefield and thought my life was done.

I speak to Ares in my thoughts, asking him to aid us if things go wrong. I again hope that he hears me and won't desert me in what could be my greatest time in need.

Maximus's stance eases, but he still trudges ahead, guarding us. Part of me worries about his safety. I have kept him shielded all these years, as he has done for me. But we are in a peculiar setting with eternal beings.

I pick up my pace, and Clotho steps in line with me. The palace entrance lies ahead. Large columns with cypress trees spaced out in between them spring up into view. Here, there are fewer mortals and more gods. Some of them wave in greeting. Clotho returns their salutations, but I simply nod and take a slight bow at the waist.

I am in an unfamiliar court of people who are not like those in Roma. I am unsure how to act, so I choose quiet courtesy while observing what's happening around me.

I am not sure if any of it matters at this point. We are here for the summons, the final judgment to prove love wins over all.

32

The God-king

Clotho

My heart races as we pass the columns to get to the throne room. Marcellus's grip is the only thing keeping me steady. All around us are the immortals of this sphere, their godly eyes watching us with cold, calculating curiosity. A muted hum of voices buzzes through the crowds, but I can still hear each one of our footsteps. Up ahead, the vast grand chamber comes into view. I quicken my pace, ready to get this ordeal over with.

Turbulent energies pulse through the area upon our entry. Immediately, I spot the god-king: Zeus sits straight-backed upon a large, gold throne, radiating vitality and raw power. He possesses an imposing strength akin to his father, Cronos. I had never sensed the similarity before until I was in that cavern with the old Titan. I shrink down as his icy stare sweeps the room and almost stop myself from proceeding further.

Zeus's entire countenance is something to behold, like the deceptive serenity before a raging storm. Draped over his large muscular frame, he wears an azure chlamys gathered at the right shoulder with a luminous golden eagle brooch securing it in place. Wheat-blond locks spiral down in perfect waves around his shoulders. But the most striking thing about his appearance is the electric blue of his eyes. As he looks down at our group, his irises shift like the changing skies to a tumultuous gray and I swear I see them flash with light.

"Come forward, Clotho and company. The time of deliberation is now." His voice rumbles as he beckons us to come closer.

His looming presence intensifies as he sits on his throne, positioned high above the other seats in the area. Gilded, etched steps lead up to his lofty perch overlooking the main floor. Below him, the other eleven Olympians encircle him in small silver chairs.

I scan each one sitting in their seat as their gazes wash over me. One pair of eyes cuts through the rest like a light in the darkest cave, guiding me out: Hades's stare meets mine with familiar warmth and compassion. While the others look on with cold indifference, I see nothing but comfort and assurance in the pools of his dark green eyes. His ghostly pallor and flowing jet-black hair create a striking juxtaposition to his brother Zeus. Yet there is something comforting in his gaze that centers me. Even as the gravity of the situation hangs over me.

Concern furrows his brow. Not for himself, but for me. I glance over to the other gods seated by him and spot Ares. He is also quite the opposite of his father, with thick sepia locks wildly spiraling to his wide shoulders. He wears his favorite bronzed armor encrusted with red rubies across the chest plate. He shifts restlessly in his seat, his gaze drawn to Marcellus.

It holds an intensity that gives me pause. Ares studies my love further, but the look on Ares's face is not cruel or cold like the others. It seems personal. There is also something soft despite his fierce presence. A protectiveness swirls in his eyes, and I look to Marcellus, wondering if there is something about him that I have missed. Something guarded by the God of War himself.

Ares shoots a glance in my direction. His eyes seem to tell me *stop*, and I do. I file my thoughts away and stand with Marcellus and my sisters surrounding me. Maximus sits in front of us, yet he remains on guard, ever observant of the happenings around him.

Zeus looms over us from his grand pedestal. The room buzzes with what sounds like a thousand hushed voices as we hold our breath, waiting for the god-king to continue. My eyes scan the meticulously decorated room once more. Ornate frescoes hang on the walls. Beneath our feet is polished marble laced with gold on the floor. Everything is impeccable, right down to the draperies.

This great hall is meant to be just as imposing as Zeus. He notes my awe and smirks, his attention locking onto me. "You dare to bring this human before me after what you've done? Brave little Fate, aren't you?" His words crack through the air as thunderous as Cronos's. Every tongue stills, and all eyes are on him.

Placidity descends in the wake of Zeus's booming voice. I shudder beneath the weight of it, knowing what sort of energy he is flinging in my direction. I almost fear speaking but know I must rise to meet his challenge.

Steeling myself, I step forward and reply, "I did as you asked, and I will not part from my eternal companion."

Zeus scoffs at my words, but the other gods chatter amongst themselves. Some seem sympathetic to my words.

His rich voice echoes against the walls once more. "And what of the cosmic balance? You disturbed the natural order by defying Fate's designations by combining threads, going against my rule."

"An outdated rule," Hades interjects.

"Seal your lips, Brother. How do I know their puppy love hasn't clouded their better judgments?" Zeus says.

"Our love is true, and we both proved it." I press back.

"Yet at what cost? Cronos has altered Aetheria forever, and it's all because of you."

"I can easily admit my mistake," I say. "I knew what I was doing when I tampered with Marcellus's thread mixing my own with his, but have we not made a quick resolution on our end? Cronos has been dealt with?"

"Has he? I know he looms over Tartarus, but not within its walls. He needs to return immediately, but my sentries tell me you made him a promise."

"That I did. Did it not quell his chaos? You gave me no direction on how to handle him, so I did what I had to."

"At what cost? Tell us now." Zeus's voice booms through the hall as he sweeps out his arms in a grand gesture.

I know he is doing this to intimidate, but I stand still as the crowds below hum in mass, I can hear many calling out to answer the question.

"Cronos would like to have Tartarus as his boon. He will leave this world of ours alone and not assault it further once this is done. I see no reason you can't do this."

The sounds of voices buzz and escalate, growing increasingly louder and more chaotic. My revelation has shocked everyone present, but I will not waver in my promise to Cronos.

"And you thought it wise to give in to this demand?" Zeus says in disbelief, his eyes growing wide despite his thundering tone.

"Yes, what do we have to lose? He is in a humbled state, and reasonable, unlike you," I snap.

"Cronos, reasonable? Have you hit your head?"

"Zeus, I will not play games. You tasked me with stopping Cronos. I did. Now we make good on our bargain. If you wanted him dealt with in a certain way, you had every opportunity to tell me what you needed me to do. *You didn't*. Instead, you sent Minos the Devil to deal with us. You had Carya try to seduce Marcellus. All those stupid little games for what? All because I dare to love a mortal?"

"And so, you think a lowly goddess like yourself is allowed to make such a weighted decision on Aetheria's behalf?"

"You didn't do it, so I had to. I did what I thought was the right thing. You want the Titans to stay in Tartarus? I gave you that. What's the problem?" I ask.

"You made a promise I feel I cannot keep as a king," Zeus says.

"So, you'd let Aetheria descend back into madness because you cannot let go of the past? Move on from this. Show us you are a fair king."

"Nothing about that promise is fair. Cronos will surely betray you. He will betray us all. Even a small taste of that kind of power drives him to lunacy," Zeus says.

"Then safeguard the outside barriers of Tartarus. If any pass without permission, they face our courts and justice. You are acting like there are no solutions."

Athena stands and agrees. "She is right, Father. If it will stop the Titans from interceding, I vote keep the promise and lay the boundaries. It's simple, and it makes more sense than our previous failed attempts. This is the answer we've been seeking for so long."

"Aye!" others shout.

"Silence!" Zeus bellows; then he mutters under his breath about me. I can sense the anger he holds, and his disdain for me is building by the second. "I have final say, and I won't keep this promise."

I have no idea how to counter his words. Athena is one of his wisest council members, and he often values her word above all. The fact she agrees speaks volumes. Why can't he see reason?

A tense hush falls over the hall, the atmosphere growing unnaturally still as the encroaching silence drowns whispered voices out. The torches on the walls flicker and dim as a chill reverberates around. As shadows seep in around the edges, the room gradually loses its brightness. All eyes turn toward the back. A tall, cloaked figure emerges, the darkness following him in his wake.

My brother is here.

"We thought you might say that," Thanatos utters, his voice carrying the haunting chorus of a thousand lost souls. Uneasy murmurs slip through the throngs, but Zeus remains stoic on his throne, regarding the God of Death with a piercing gaze.

Zeus's lip twitches. "What is this? Do you believe your brother will force my hand? My mind remains unchanged." He scoffs.

Thanatos raises his gloved hand, revealing a thick golden thread resting in his palm. "Is that so?"

33

The Golden Thread

Clotho

"Do you know whose thread I hold in my hands, god-king?" Thanatos asks.

Zeus straightens on his throne, a flash of uncertainty in his eyes. Even from here, I can see his jaw tighten and twitch at the corner of his mouth. My brother smirks and fixes his gaze onto him. Under the full force of Thanatos' stare, Zeus shifts almost imperceptibly in his seat.

He is unsettled by Death itself, giving Atropos time to whip out her favorite shears. They are small and fit in her palm. If he fights us on the terms once more, we will be ready.

"Answer me, Zeus," my brother says.

A clap of thunder shakes the hall as Zeus rises from his throne. "I will not be manipulated. The thread you hold means nothing to me without context."

"You'd have me explain when you already know? Come now, it's yours. We hold the threads of all beings, immortal, mortal, and otherwise. Pray tell, what will you do now?"

Zeus smirks. "Careful, I am still king. This is treason."

"Careful, or we will show why you do not tamper with Death and Fate incarnate." Thanatos turns to Atropos, who holds the shears wide open around the thread.

"I beg you all to tread lightly."

"And we implore you to see reason for once and follow through with our plan. Again, you sent Clotho to tame Cronos without a single word of advice from you. If you wanted a different outcome, you shouldn't have sat on your throne sending out others to do your dirty work." Thanatos's words sting as Zeus remains silent.

"Even now, you're silent, wanting to shut us down. Athena herself said this is a better course of action," I interject.

The other eleven converse quietly amongst themselves. Athena stands again. "Father, you need to follow through with this. We watched the mortal Marcellus pass each test, and Clotho did as she was asked. Stop this madness. If this strategy has a way of creating peace with the Titans, let's do it. Please see reason and step back. You are still our king. Nothing changes that."

"They would betray me to get what they want," he growls.

Athena states bluntly, "What they want is freedom to choose whom they love and to stop Cronos from inserting himself in Aetheria. It all makes sense. You, yourself, have many children that are half-mortal. Stop using humans as your playthings while making other immortals pay for falling in love with them."

"We chose this because we already knew what your answer would be. You are too close to the situation to see outside of it like others do. Cronos is your father, after all," I add.

Zeus's face turns a dark shade of red, anger boiling up faster than I've seen in Ares.

"Fine, but if Cronos turns against this, you will be punished."

Lachesis steps forward. "We accept that. We've told you we will personally deal with the Titan if he tries anything that goes against the deal made."

"And what of Marcellus and Clotho?" Athena asks. "Will you leave them alone to live out their lives in peace?"

"Yes. I don't know why you suddenly care so much, Daughter," Zeus grumbles.

"Because we need to stop devaluing other immortals, particularly the ones who oversee life and death itself."

Zeus surveys the thread in Thanatos's hands once more. "Very well, I relent. We will follow through with your promise to the old Titan."

"And we will continue to obey Fate's design. You know what has occurred was already set in the great weave," Thanatos replies calmly.

"Will you grant Clotho and Marcellus peace now?" Lachesis asks.

Zeus scowls but nods curtly. "They may go. But do not presume this challenges my authority."

"As you say, Father. Shall we put this matter to rest and focus on preserving order?" Athena interjects diplomatically.

Zeus's anger still brews beneath the surface. But the others have spoken and made it clear what will happen next. "The arrangement stands but know this: I will be watching Tartarus closely."

I let out a sigh of relief. Marcellus thanks the gods with a bow, and Zeus dismisses us in a cold manner. I take Marcellus's hand in mine, but the tension still lingers in the air. Maximus lets out a low whine before we turn to walk away.

There is something churning in my gut as our backs now face the god-king. I don't want to make a show of distrust, so I continue walking out the way we came in. Atropos links arms with me, and we are almost at the exit when thunder claps and a flash of blinding light overwhelms everything around me.

34
Lightning
Clotho

I am surrounded by chaos. Lightning streaks wildly across the hall, scorching marble columns that groan under the pressure of the strikes and crumble around the edges—threatening to collapse on top of us. Even the floor trembles under the fury of Zeus's power. Throngs of immortals rush out, tumbling over one another as they seek safety above all else.

Howling winds whip through the room, sending the remaining bodies into walls. I scramble up, searching for my love, and spot him on the ground. A bloodcurdling scream drowns out all other sounds. *It is mine.*

I reach out, hands shaking uncontrollably, as I grab Marcellus, my fingers desperately seeking a pulse, for any sign that he is alive and well. But the raging ener-

gies crackle and surge, making my skin crawl and my head spin. A guttural cry rips from my throat.

"No, please, my love," I beg, clutching Marcellus tight enough to feel the expansion of his ribs with each precious breath. Relief crashes through my entire being in a dizzying wave.

He is alive.

My thumbs brush his temples as I clutch his face, sobbing while I press my forehead to his. *My heart.* The heat of his breath warms my face as I wrap myself around him, enveloping him like a shield with my body. His arms encircle my waist. Further relief washes over me when I hear him whisper in my ear, "I'm all right."

I turn my eyes upward, and Ares stands with his shield up and spear at the ready.

Marcellus and I make our way to our feet and hold on to each other. There is a moment of silence before Ares's voice echoes through the hall.

"You will not strike down my son!" he says.

The room fills with loud gasps, and Zeus rushes down to meet his son one on one. "Lies! This man is mortal. I do not sense a shred of Olympian in him."

"Why would I lie? What do I gain?" Ares's spear meets Zeus's chin. The two are at an impasse.

"Explain yourself now," Zeus growls, his right hand engulfed in tiny electrical sparks. A jagged sword appears, and he meets Ares's spear with a loud clang.

Ares pushes back. "I do not wish to fight my own father, but I will if I must."

Zeus's voice grows quiet. "Give me the answers I seek."

"Stay your hand, Father. I will tell you what you need to know."

"Then I will ask you to do the same. Put down your spear and we shall converse without force."

My eyes dart anxiously between Zeus and Ares. The tension in the air is so thick that I swear it could be cut with a knife. They stare each other down without a single blink of an eye. Both still have their weapons poised — ready to be used. One false move could unleash catastrophe.

The standoff has no end in sight. Every passing second frays my nerves. I hold Marcellus close, waiting for one of them to break.

Ares breaks the silence. "I need you to promise that Marcellus will remain untouched."

Zeus relents. "Fine, we will do it your way." His sword dissipates into thin air.

Ares lays down his spear and sighs. "Hecate helped me hide his true demi-god status, for protection, and for Marcellus to experience true free will. I did not want your influence upon him. I also wanted him to prove himself on his merits, not his father's."

The fleeting vision of Hecate in that cave flashes through my memory. She was there to aid her follower, Marcellus's mother and Ares's secret mortal lover.

"How was his thread not detected? Clotho, I need answers now!" Zeus looks at me, demanding an answer.

I let out a sigh of exasperation and retort, "Are you *not* aware that only gods' threads are different? Demi-god or mortal, the strings are all the same."

I cannot believe the god-king is asking these types of questions. My sisters and I have frequently discussed that kind of information. This proves he doesn't take our stations seriously as he should. I keep my composure despite wanting to call him out for ignoring the very basics of what the Fates do.

“And nothing about his life made you question if he was more than mortal? Were you aware that Hecate was involved?” he asks.

I give Zeus a pointed glare, lips pressed thin in irritation. “No, I know how to mind my own business, unlike some other immortals in the room.”

“So you knew something happened at his birth with the old goddess?”

“Yes.” I cross my arms and wait for him to interrogate me further.

He raises his brow. “And you didn’t think to mention this earlier?”

I scoff. He acts like he would have let me speak to him prior to this situation. “Zeus, you know as well as I do that messing with a goddess far older and wiser is foolhardy at best. Her secrets are hers to keep and not mine to indulge.” My words bite with disdain as I throw my hands up in irritation.

“Still, nothing tempted you to seek more information?”

"No, I do not see every single moment in a person's life, just enough, and even then, the threads I weave provide many choices and varying outcomes. You should already know this? Why do I need to clarify?" I ask.

"You are correct and make valid points. I have no further queries. Not even I will tangle with the goddess Hecate, I know better, but you, my son." Zeus turns and points his finger at Ares. "Tell me now, where is this lover?"

"Why does this matter?" Ares asks.

"I would like to meet this woman and decide for myself whether she is worthy of my son." Zeus's tone drips with deception.

Ares shifts his feet and readies himself for the worst. "So now you wish to harm another innocent person? I am not telling you anything more."

Zeus's face flashes with golden light. "Tell me now or suffer the consequences. I will send you packing to Tartarus myself."

Ares sighs. "I knew you'd use that as a threat. Have it your way, then." Ares stalls, a smirk curling on his lips.

"Spit it out!"

"Fortunately, she is somewhere safe, and you are too late. There is nothing you can say or do to affect her."

Marcellus balls up his fist. "Fortunately? My mother is dead! How can you say you even loved her?" He staggers back, like Ares's words are a physical blow. I reach my hand to take his and he grasps onto it. His entire body is shaking, but Ares remains calm.

"Marcellus, I promise you I love your mother, and she is well." Ares's voice softens, his usual arrogant tone gone. "Death is not the end. Bellona is in the Elysium Fields. Zeus cannot touch her, and when I fully restore your demi-god status, you can travel there to see her like I do."

"Such foolish notions, Ares, I forbid this," Zeus intercepts. "Your secrets have cost you. I will not allow you or Marcellus entrance to the Underworld again."

Hades steps down, walking slowly to Ares and Zeus. "Is that so, Brother? You dare to claim you have reign over my domain?"

I grab Marcellus and pull him closer and mutter, "Stay close, don't move."

Whatever is about to happen, it will not be pretty. Zeus has clearly lost it. It is one thing for him to claim the title god-king, but the Underworld belongs to Hades.

"I will not have my son and brother usurp me!" Zeus bellows, hardening his stance.

Hades cracks his neck to the side, his words clipped and final. "And you will not force your rule on my realm. You have no rights, and I will stop you right here without a second thought."

Ares reacts next with blurring speed, picking up his spear. Hades's eyes flicker with blue flames and shadowy blades form in his hands. Zeus's weapon reappears and bolts of light blaze across his flesh. All three of them are prepared to go head-to-head. I cannot believe what is happening in front of me. I usher Marcellus and my sisters back. Atropos whispers, "We still have his thread, say the words, I will unravel a small string of it. This will stop him."

"No," I tell her.

"Why?"

I point to the silver chairs on the rise as Athena and Hera descend from their seats. "We have no need with so many on our side."

Athena leaps down the steps with ease and lands between brothers, father, and son. "Stay your weapons!" she commands. "This conflict serves no purpose when we already have the solution at hand!"

Ares hesitates and stands back, but Zeus snarls, "You dare to interfere?"

"I dare to speak wisdom yet again," she replies evenly. "I am disappointed in your actions, Father. Please, let us keep to the agreement."

Hera joins Athena's side, laying a restraining hand on Zeus's arm. "Be still, my husband. Surely, we can resolve this without more contention. Please, listen to your children, if not for my sake, for them. You are walking a fine line, much like your father did. Stop this madness before you become him."

Zeus shrugs off her touch, but he pauses, the lightning that flashed across his skin fading.

Hades steps forward. "Give Marcellus the chance to live. I will deal with my kingdom on my own terms and take your counsel into consideration."

Zeus scowls, grumbling. "I will allow Marcellus to live, under one condition. Ares is banned from the Underworld for two thousand years."

Athena looks to Ares; the pain of sadness fills his eyes, but without hesitation he says, "I accept your terms, Father."

Marcellus glances at me, his eyes widen in shock. I raise my eyebrows. I am stunned by the turn of events. Never in all my immortal years would I have imagined the proud and bloody God of War to be capable of such a selfless sacrifice on behalf of his half-mortal son. I would have never guessed the ferocity of his fatherly bond since he kept his distance and Marcellus a secret.

I am awestruck by Ares's act of grace. Marcellus is speechless. He looks at Ares and then back at me, searching my face. I nod in Ares's direction and guide him over to where his true father stands.

Ares turns to Zeus. "Are we done here? Can Clotho and my son leave without further harassment from you?"

"Yes, they can leave. But one misstep from you and I may go back on my promise."

"Then it is done. You are still king. We will leave you to begin preparations for Tartarus," Ares says.

"Marcellus, are you okay?" Ares asks.

He stares up at Ares. I try to read his expression, but I can't.

"I–I think so."

"The two of you need to go. I will come find you both and we will talk. I promise you that, my son." Ares takes Marcellus into a hug, and now the entire court of the gods gape in shock. Marcellus tenses up and I can see a pained look on Ares's face before he speaks again.

"I will also remove the veil that hangs over you now. The one that hid your demi-god status all these years."

Marcellus shakes his head, the revelation that he is the son of a god still baffles him. "What... what do you mean?" he stammers.

"When you were born, Hecate placed a veil over you to protect you from other immortals and hide your true nature. Only she or I can withdraw this shroud. After today, you will need to embrace all your power. It will allow you to stay on the Mounts as long as you like and to travel through the Underworld unscathed."

Marcellus speaks in low, even tones, "I understand. Do what you must."

"I am relieved to hear this. I would converse further, but you really should go. I want you both safe and happy." He smiles and reaches out to Marcellus but pulls himself back.

"I am sorry. I know you don't see me as Father, but I have watched over you since birth. Every minute I could spare, I was there with you."

Marcellus takes a step closer to his father and shakes his hand. Ares seems to accept this.

"Now go." He shuffles us both out of the hall.

"When will we see you?" Marcellus asks.

"In an hour or two. Clotho, go to your cabin and stay there with him."

"It will be done," I reply.

We take our leave, heading back through the city. The clouds in the sky have lifted, and warm sunlight dances across our faces. I take a deep breath and release it. Peace overcomes me. We are free from Zeus and anyone who wished to assault us further.

I am excited for what lies ahead.

In this moment, all feels right in the world. Our love weathered the storm and opened the doors for others to love freely, as we do.

Hands clasped tight together, Marcellus and I walk to the bridge that leads to the Mount my family and I live on. Marcellus stops and smiles, squeezing my hand. "I am excited to see your home," he says.

Lachesis and Atropos run ahead, leaving laughter in their wake. Thanatos saunters behind us, a deep grin on his face. I love this little family of mine. They all stood beside me when it mattered.

"Thank you all again for everything."

"What is family for? What would our bond be worth if we hadn't supported you, little sister?" Thanatos questions.

"We'd have nothing," I reply.

"Exactly. And we are not like the other immortals on the Mounts. We have not let our immortality twist us to feel nothing."

"I agree." I smile.

Atropos and Lachesis come skipping back. They speak in unison. "And we value family above all else."

"Yes, thank you, all of you," Marcellus says.

"You are family too." Thanatos pats Marcellus on the back. I can see the hairs on his neck stand up.

"Brother!" my sisters and I shout in unison.

"What?" he shrugs.

"You're making him uncomfortable." I chide gently.

"Oh, I forgot. Death's touch." Thanatos laughs.

Marcellus eases up a bit, running his hand through his hair. "I have to admit, that was a bit unsettling."

"In time, you will get used to it." I wink.

The sun dips low on the horizon, painting the land in hues of oranges, magentas, and golds. I press the group to continue onward. "We should get ourselves home as quickly as possible. I am sure everyone wants dinner."

"Oh yes! Does this mean you and Marcellus are going to cook?" Atropos is giddy with excitement.

Lachesis agrees. "They better. Thanatos, you missed out on the most amazing feast created by these two."

All three chatter some more, getting ahead of us. I slow down, and Marcellus wraps one arm around my waist before pulling me in for a kiss.

We stop for a moment. Whatever mystery our future holds, we can face it together. There is a certain excitement that fills my being for what is coming.

I can't wait to see how life unfolds. I want to bring some of my threads down to his farm. Maybe we can spend summers on the Mounts and winters down on Aetheria. I won't stay secluded anymore. I want to visit Karnak, or travel to the Isle of Norn. The possibilities are endless, and the rest of our lives are just beginning.

35

A Veil Removed

Marcellus

We arrive at Clotho's home. This is the house she shares with her sisters. The terrain here is so different from the world below. There are wildflowers everywhere, of every shade of color. Massive mushrooms the size of a barn cat dot the mossy ground beneath giant oak trees that shade one side of the cabin. Tangled ivy vines up the weather-worn walls and a stone chimney peeks out from a sloped shingled roof.

Clotho gestures for me to enter. I go to step in, but Maximus barrels past me before I can move. Barking happily, he plops down on the thick wool rug near the fireplace and settles in. All of us are laughing. I stride in next, and the inside somehow seems much larger than what appeared on the outside. She shows

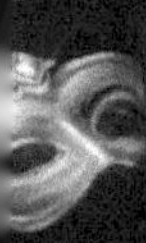

me around. There are neat piles of threads on a single table. The smell of rosemary, lavender, and sage hangs heavy in the air. Dried herbs hang near a window draped with purple silk. There are many tinctures in glass bottles corked up, waiting to be used.

A stark contrast to Zeus and the city of Olympus.

A small fire crackles in the hearth as Clotho leads me around, showing me each room. Everything is simple, yet elegant in its own way. Lachesis and Atropos are at the kitchen table chopping up vegetables.

"That entire ordeal has me hungrier than a horse!" Atropos squeaks.

"I agree with you there, Sister," Lachesis says.

Clotho pulls out some flour and beckons me to her, and we do what we do best. Make dinner.

The simple stew and bread we worked up now fills my belly. I wait for Ares as we all sit by the fire. I thought early spring in Roma was chilly, but I was wrong. I take advantage of the cold and hold Clotho tight. My fingers comb through her hair as I revel in her closeness. There's a sense of relief that washes over me after enduring what we have.

A low rap at the door causes me to spring to my feet, instantly alert. I head to the door and Clotho joins me. For a split second, I look at her and she nods.

I crack it open and there stands my father. It is strange to me. He has been my patron god for so long, and while I know he has been there for me, the idea that he is my parent hasn't settled within me.

"Hello Marcellus. Are you ready?" he asks.

"I think so, but first, can I ask some questions?"

"Of course."

"I think I understand why you shielded me as you did, but why did you let my mother die?"

"We knew it was the only way we could truly be together. Hades isn't as unreasonable as he's made out to be."

"I guess I thought death was more permanent, like my family is gone and I cannot be with them."

"Your mother is not just a mortal, and she didn't die a natural death, so to speak. She is also a demi-god, so the rules are different. Life spans are too."

"What are you saying?"

"She chose to go to the Underworld. Zeus was close to finding out about her, about you. You and Cecelia had just had little Marcella, too. We couldn't risk all of you. I know none of this makes sense. We wanted to keep everyone safe."

"I have seen the raw power of the gods. I think I understand."

While I can follow his reasoning, everything he tells me weighs me down. There is so much I didn't know. The heavy burden my mother carried. They both believed they were protecting me. I am not sure I can be angry with either of them.

"I realize now that we should have told you. I'm so sorry. Again, we wanted to protect you."

"You have my thanks. There is no need to apologize. I have made difficult decisions as a father, as a husband," I say.

Ares seems shocked. "Truly?"

"Yes."

"Then let us do this. Remove the veil."

"Wait," I hold up my hand. "Is there any pain involved? Anything I should be aware of?"

"No, it is simple. You will feel something, but it won't be as painful as a battle wound."

I chuckle. "Good to know. What else can you tell me? I don't feel ready."

I am not prepared by any means, but he clarifies the reason to say yes. "Zeus is unaware, but with your mother being demi-god as well. You have more Olympian in your blood than most. It will help you in the years to come. If I had known he was sending Minos after you, I would have told you sooner and offered to lift it immediately. By the time I was told, it was too late, but as always, you proved yourself as mortal. You are ready for this. All your achievements are your own." He pauses. "Marcellus, you have done well, my son, but once this veil lifts you will be more, you will be whole. Do you understand?"

I ponder for a moment. My mother was a demi-god, too—this is news! I have more questions, but there is time to get the answers later. I also have my doubts about Zeus. I cannot trust his word since he back-tracked so easily. If this assists me in making sure we get to be together, then I need to do this.

"Admittedly, I have more questions, but you can answer later. I think I am ready. Let's do this." Clotho takes my hand in hers and I wait for Ares to do whatever it is he must do.

"Here," Ares says, pointing to a chair at the kitchen table. "You should sit down for this." He pulls the chair out and positions it out in the open.

"Clotho, you can stand close. Your sisters are welcome too." He motions for them to join us. Atropos and Lachesis stand near Clotho, encircling the chair I take a seat in.

Ares stands behind me, his hands placed on my shoulders. "Are you ready?"

"I am."

His grip tightens on me as he chants. "Spáse ta desmá soun, yié tou theoú. Apokálypse tin alithiní sou morphí, gie tou Áris ris. As fanerothí i theïkí sou dýnami se ólo tis to megalío. Tóra!"

A sharp twinge hits every nerve and muscle in my body. I flex my hands as a tingling sensation overcomes every inch of me. My legs and arms twitch. Heat builds in my shoulders, traveling to my hands and into my neck, then down into my chest. It's like

I have a sudden fever. Sweat gathers on my brow as I struggle to breathe in and out.

Clotho shifts forward but stops herself. She glances up at Ares. It seems an unspoken understanding passes between them as she bows her head and takes a step back.

He repeats the words again:

"Spáse ta desmá soun, yié tou theoú. Apokálypse tin alithiní sou morphí, gie tou Áris ris. As fanerothí i theïkí sou dýnami se ólo tis to megalío. Tóra!"

At first, I do not understand the ancient tongue in which he speaks, but as he cites it again, I hear him clearly:

Break these bonds, son of a god. Reveal your true form, son of Ares. Let your divine power be made manifest in all its greatness. As I will, it is done!

As Ares chants the incantation a third time, a blaze of energy surges through me. My nerves are on fire this time and I shake. He takes hold of me, wrapping his arms around me across my chest. Wave after wave of searing energy keeps the convulsions coming, my body temperature still rising. I cannot stop it. I gasp for air as the cascading force of the veil lifting overcomes me.

Ares stays calm. "Clotho, come help me hold him steady. Breathe, my son, breathe."

She bends down and wraps herself around my waist as they both hold me still. Her gentle touch does something, and I catch my breath. The heat dissipates, leaving my body soaked in sweat. A chill races across my damp skin, making me shiver all over.

Atropos springs into action. I see her shoot across the room outside of my view. She comes back with a blanket. Lachesis grabs one side and helps drape it over me. Clotho grabs a cloth, wiping my face gently. Ares still holds onto my shoulders. Everything around me intensifies, but I try to relax with the thought that I am surrounded by people who care for me.

My senses sharpen further. I perceive minute details I didn't before. Up in the shadowed rafters I spot a delicate spider spinning a tiny intricate web while specks of dust in the air catch the firelight, swirling in a dance only visible to sharpened eyes. Their waltz has me mesmerized. Colors shine more brightly, revealing new dimensions and depth I never noticed before.

The room remains the same, yet every scent, texture, and object has transformed, each facet illuminated in profound detail. I gaze at Clotho, and she shines brighter than anything else. I see a silken silver thread for a mere second from the center of my chest leading to hers, glittering in the fire's light. I watch it fade, but I am now more aware of how bonded we truly are. Our souls have been tied together since the beginning.

This revelation makes my heart swell. I take Clotho's hand and pull myself up to stand next to her. Overwhelmed by lightheadedness, I cling to her for support as my body sways uncontrollably until I find my balance. Ares is also right there, helping her, and it gives me a sense of peace knowing that I have a father I can connect with. "Are you all right?" he asks. "Lachesis, can you grab him a cup of water?"

Lachesis wastes no time in filling a stone cup and brings it to me. "Thank you." I muster, putting the cool rim to my mouth and taking a sip with Clotho's assistance.

Clotho strokes my temples with her soft fingers and looks deeply into my eyes. "Oh, my love. I am here.

We are here for you. You are my heart's string. Your wellbeing means everything to me."

I bring her palm to my lips, kissing it softly. "You are my world. The other half of my soul. I love you beyond words of life itself."

She pulls me close, and I rest my head on hers. "Thank you, thank you all." I breathe.

Ares speaks next. "You are whole, my son. I am done here. If you wish, I can take my leave."

"No, stay awhile longer," I tell him.

And he does for a bit. The five of us gather around the fire—speaking of simpler times and hopes for the future to come. There is still much to mend. If we are called to fix small matters on Aetheria, I am more than ready to aid its people.

As the embers burn low, Ares bids us farewell. Clotho and I retreat to her bed, curled up in each other's arms. Outside, night's lullaby strums away on cricket's wings and I am comforted by the chapter we've added to our evolving story. There will be time enough to write the next when dawn's first light wakes us.

36

Looking to the Future

Clotho

Dawn's rosy light streams in through the curtain's cracks, creeping along the walls. I slide carefully from our shared bed, letting Marcellus rest. The night is over, and our tribulations are at an end, but there is much to be done.

I stand outside, relishing the cool morning air. The breeze whispers through the trees, beckoning the sleeping world to wake up with me. Somewhere deep within, I hear a faint hum of Destiny calling. Our next chapter is about to unfold.

I hear a deep yawn and glance back to see Marcellus stretching his arms up and out. He comes to my side. This is the first day of what feels like a new beginning. No hiding our love for each other, no running from enemies who wish to harm us. I take in the scene sur-

rounding us. Delicate flowers gently unfurl with dewdrops still clinging to their petals. The birds' melodic calls ring out, echoing through the small wood encircling the cabin.

The growing sunlight brings out chattering squirrels while the last of the nocturnal animals head to their burrows. Marcellus caresses my waist and kisses my cheek. "What comes next?" he asks.

"I have threads to spin, but first, breakfast."

He chuckles and takes my hand in his, heading back inside.

Plans unfold over hot tea, biscoctus, and cheese filled crepes. We still plan to split our time between the Mount and farm, but we both agree to let things unfold naturally and vow to live a little, go with the flow being inspired by the divine energies that course around our world. Whatever adventures calls us next, we will follow.

Despite the rough beginning, things have come together unexpectedly, and I love how we work together in synergy as a couple. Marcellus busies himself around our humble abode, tidying up our workspaces while I clean the dishes from breakfast. I can't help but grin as Maximus trots behind him. That dog has a special place in my heart and always will.

Later, Lachesis and Atropos work on a permanent portal to avoid wasting time traveling to either. In hindsight, I should have asked them to help with something like this earlier. I try to afford myself some grace. Love has a way of taking all rationality away. Yet, I do not think I would have it any other way.

Even though I have lived a thousand years, there is always a lesson to be learned. Information to be gleaned from each situation. And more to explore, more of life to be experienced.

I know I would change nothing about our journey so far. Afternoon sunlight filters through the leaves, dappling us both with light and shadow. Looking at Marcellus, I know I am where I belong. We walk holding hands and I can't help but think: A blank page and a bottle of ink are waiting for us to start the next chapter.

Whatever is written in the stars, no matter what happens next. Our story is far from over. One thing I know without a shred of doubt, we will always have each other.

The End.

Note from the Author

When I began writing Cursed by Fate, I was inspired by Greek mythology and a simple 'what if?'. The story itself reimagines many elements for a fresh take on the gods and goddess of old. This is where the reader finds themselves transported to the fictional world of Aetheria and not ancient Greece. The goal was to breathe new life into these myths that have endured a millennia in a way that speaks to modern audiences—opening up new perspectives on long-standing archetypes.

Maybe Destiny allows for choice and Death can represent transition rather than an end. I also value the idea of no single person being perfect, but rather perfectly imperfect, and we see this with Clotho and her decisions despite her immortal status. I also believe in true love at any age. The kind that feels epic and destined, even with life's challenges. The type of love that sees beyond the surface to find the matching rhythm with another's heart.

love always,

Adalynd

Glossary

Aetheria - (ee-THEER-ee-uh) - The world where Cursed by Fate takes place.

Amphinome - (am-FIN-oh-mee) - One of the nereid sisters who helps Marcellus.

Arcadia - (ar-KAY-dee-uh) - A city in Roma on the continent of Aetheria.

Atropos - (A-tro-pos) - One of the Three Fates. She cuts the threads of life.

Biscoctus – (Bis-cot-tus): Ancient roman term for biscotto. The singular term for a dry biscuit. Americans often call it biscotti but that is the plural form in Italian.

Cecilia - (seh-SEE-lee-uh)–Marcellus's deceased wife.

Cerberus - (SUR-bur-uhs) - The three-headed dog that guards the entrance to the Underworld.

Chimera (ki-MEER-ah)- a monster with the head of a lion, body of a goat and tail of serpent.

Clotho - (KLOH-thoh) - one of the Three Fates. She spins the threads of life.

Cronos - (KROH-nohs) - A titan, father of Zeus.

Dyname - (DIN-uh-mee) - One of the nereid sisters who helps Marcellus.

Gérontos eídōlon ep'emoi kalýptō - loosely based on Greek language and means veil an aged image over me. Essentially this a glamor spell that Clotho casts over herself.

Grecia - (GREH-see-uh)- A country in Aetheria that shares a border with Roma.

Hades - (HAY-deez) - God of the Underworld.

Iaso - (eye-AY-soh) - Goddess of healing and remedies.

Kharon - (KHAIR-uhn) - Ferryman who transports souls to the Underworld.

Lachesis - (La-KUH-sis) - One of the Three Fates. She measures the threads of life.

Marcella - (mar-CEL-uh) – Marcellus's deceased daughter.

Marcellus - (mar-CELL-us) – Mortal lover of Clotho.

Maximus - (MAX-ih-muhs) – Marcellus's dog.

Minos - (MY-nohs) - A demigod son of Zeus. In some Greek myths he is good in others he is bad and thus Minos the Devil was born for this story.

Molossus- Roman war dog similar to modern day Cane Corso.

Moirai - (mwah-RY) - Another name for the Three Fates.

New Athens - A city in Aetheria.

Nymph- refers to any nature spirit. Dryads, naiads, and nereids are all different types of nymphs for example.

Persephone - (purr-SEH-fuh-nee) - Goddess of the Underworld, wife of Hades.

Phoebe - (FEE-bee) - A dressmaker in Aetheria.

Pythia - (PIH-thee-uh) - An oracle who gives Clotho a prophecy.

Roma - (ROH-muh) - A country bordering Greca.

Scylla - (SKIHL-uh) - A gigantic squid/ sea-monster.

Tartarus - (TAR-tuh-ruhs) - A prison for defeated gods and titans. But it has changed over time what was once a crumbling, decayed kingdom has been built up by Cronos and his fellow Titans.

Thanatos - (THAN-uh-tohs) - God of death, brother of Clotho.

The Floating Mounts: There are twelve distinct floating mountains amongst many others, floating high above the world of Aetheria. There are many bridges that connect the twelve together, while others float singularly in the air and have gone unexplored by mortals.

Clotho's Stew Recipe

Ingredients:

Two pounds of cubed up boneless beef chuck roast

½ teaspoon of freshly ground pepper (or to taste)

¾ teaspoon of kosher salt (or to taste)

¼ cup of olive oil/ or avocado (clarified bacon grease or beef tallow works too)

A pound and a half of whole pearl onions (frozen for ease)

Four cloves of minced garlic

4 tablespoons of tomato paste

2 to 3 large scarlet tomatoes cut-up (or alternatively use canned)

¼ teaspoon of ground allspice

1 cinnamon stick

¼ ground clove

1 teaspoon of oregano

2 bay leaves

1 cup of beef bone broth and more *as needed

One cup of full-bodied red wine

¼ cup of brandy

In a large skillet or heavy-bottom pot, sear the beef in oil of choice (or the tallow/ bacon grease). Once the meat is browned remove from pan and then add the onions. Let them cook for a few minutes before adding your spices, salt, pepper, and tomato paste. Add your meat back to the pot and stir it well, coating the meat well. Next, add your wine and brandy to help deglaze the pot. Cook briefly and stir occasionally to let the alcohol cook down. Then add your tomatoes and bone broth as needed. Now cover and let simmer on low, allowing the ingredients to mesh together and cook until the meat is tender (about an hour and forty minutes,maybe two hours). Stir halfway through and add more broth if necessary.

Before serving, remove cinnamon stick and bay leaves. Allow to sit uncovered to cool down and serve immediately.

Some notes: I am a to taste person on spices, so adjust as necessary.

Can also use chicken bone broth.

Clarified bacon fat/ grease: easy to do if you are unfamiliar. Strain the rendered bacon fat through a cheesecloth to remove solids, boil and then let cool to solidify the fat. I store it in the fridge for later use.

Books By Adalynd

All books by Adalynd can be found by visiting her website at:

www.wanderlustinktome.com/agbooks

Adalynd, also known as Alexis, writes Romantic Fantasy with a touch of darkness and varying degrees of spice. When she's not momming, she's writing, creating, gardening, DIYing, and playing her favorite video game Fallout.

Adalynd is a hoarder of craft supplies, coffee cups,and books. She loves tacos, tea, and toast (with cinnamon and sugar).

Adalynd enjoys spending time with her family and has been married to the love of her life for over sixteen years. She currently resides in the majestic state of Arizona where she enjoys the three hundred plus days of sun and endless summer.

She hopes you'll take a walk in the forest of her imagination and join her as she wanders through her worlds and stories.

Connect

There are more stories to explore in the world of Aetheria (like the three thieves) and elsewhere. I would love for you to join me as I get those ready to share. All sneak peeks will be shared with my newsletter subscribers or discord members FIRST.

I'd love to see you there.

Book Wanderers Discord:

Alexis V & Adalynd G Newsletter:

Wanderlust Ink

You can also find all my links by visiting:

linktr.ee/AdalyndGrayves

My shop with signed books and other merch can be found at:

wanderlustinktome.com/shop

www.ingramcontent.com/pod-product-compliance
Lightning Source LLC
Chambersburg PA
CBHW070547310726
48982CB00011B/1492/J

* 9 7 9 8 9 8 8 9 5 4 0 2 6 *